BROTHER WARS
CABIN ELEVEN

By Steven K. Smith

MyBoys3 Press

To my brothers of The Ritz,
those were some good times

BROTHER WARS
CABIN ELEVEN

PROLOGUE

In case we haven't met before, my name's Harry, and I'm ten.

I don't usually complain about things, but my older brother, Randy, is not a usual thing. He's thirteen and his mission in life is to torment me. He once locked me in my pitch-black dark basement with our fire-breathing furnace. Another time, he nearly killed us both by forcing me down the river in a damaged canoe.

Sure, we have occasional moments when we get along, maybe two or three times a year. I know he has the capacity to act like a normal, well-behaved person. I just don't get to see that person much. Mom says she's working hard to raise two respectable young men, but I think even she'd admit that she has her work cut out for her with Randy.

Because most of the time, life with Randy is like

living in a war zone in my own home. Of course, I realize some people actually do live in real war zones with guns and bombs and terrible stuff, so I probably shouldn't complain.

But living with Randy is like my own little war.

A brother war.

CHAPTER ONE

I slid into the seat on the bus next to Nixon. He was leaned over his backpack, searching for something.

"What are you doing?" I asked.

He didn't look up. "I have to show you something."

"Okay," I said, staring out the window. The middle school across the parking lot was letting out. I saw Randy heading our way and slid a little lower, wishing we didn't share the same bus.

"Found it!" Nixon pulled a glossy brochure from his backpack. He held it in front of my nose. "You have to read this."

It was too close to my face for me to read anything. "What is it?"

"Camp Awonjahela!"

"Awonja-whatcha?"

"A-won-ja-he-la," he repeated more slowly. "It's an old Indian word that means friendship."

"What the heck is it?"

"It's a summer camp," said Nixon. "Marcy went last year. She had the best time. I get to go this year, and my parents thought it would be more fun if I went with a friend." He looked at me, eyebrows raised expectantly. "What do you think?"

"About what?"

"Do you want to come with me?"

I looked down at the brochure. A picture of a sailboat on a lake was splashed across the front.

"I'll take that," a voice said, snatching the paper from my hands.

"Hey!" I yelled. Randy walked to the back of the bus, the camp brochure held over his head like a trophy. My brother was always stealing things from me.

"That's mine," called Nixon.

"I'll get it for you, Nix," said Marcy, following Randy down the aisle. "Don't worry."

"Thanks." Nixon sighed, turning back into his seat.

"Sorry," I said. It wasn't easy being my best friend. I was always apologizing for Randy's behavior. I often wondered what it would be like to have a nice sister like Marcy. She and Randy had been dating off and on the last few months. It was off and on because it usually only took a few weeks for Randy to do something really stupid that made Marcy come to her senses for a while. Why she kept making up with him was beyond me since Marcy seems like a really smart girl. I figure Randy must be one of the luckiest guys around to get so many chances. If I were Marcy, I would have dumped him for good a long time ago.

"I guess you'll just have to tell me about the camp," I said.

Nixon's face brightened. "It'll be great, Harry. It's six days in the Adirondack mountains, and they have a big lake, boats, campouts, archery, even a rifle range."

I'd never tried to shoot a bow and arrow, or a rifle, but both sounded cool. I'd also never been away from home for a whole week before. Sure, I'd slept over at Nixon's house a bunch of times, but that's just down the street. If anything ever went wrong, I could walk back home. But at camp, a lot of things could happen and I would be stuck there. I could get sick, or there might be a tornado, or what if I woke up in the middle of the night and didn't remember where I was?

Who knows, maybe I'm just paranoid from living with Randy for all these years. But in my opinion it's always good to think through what might go wrong so you can be prepared. That's what my teacher always says we should do, although I don't know if she is talking about sleepovers.

The more Nixon told me about the camp, however,

the less I worried about sleeping away from home. As soon as I got off the bus, I ran home to ask my mom.

"So, can I go?" I asked, after I'd shared the details.

"Are you sure you can handle that, Frog Legs?" said Randy from the other side of the kitchen.

I hated it when he called me that name, but I'd pretty much stopped arguing about it. When you have a brother like Randy, you have to choose your battles.

"Randy, what have I told you about calling your brother that name?" Mom scolded.

Randy just chuckled, his usual, sinister grin on his face.

"I'll have to ask your father," said Mom. "He gets home on Wednesday."

Like usual, Dad was away on a business trip. This time he was in Milwaukee, which I think is in Wisconsin, or maybe Michigan. I'm not sure.

"Can't we just call him?" I asked. I've never been to Milwaukee, but I'm pretty sure Dad's phone should still work there. It's not like one of those faraway places where you have to get special cell service.

"Summer camp is expensive, Harry."

"But it sounds really fun," I whined.

"I agree," said Mom, "but we want to make sure he's in the right frame of mind to say yes. It's better to ask in person."

"Nixon's parents are letting him go," I said, flopping

down into the kitchen chair as Mom chopped a carrot. "In fact, they're paying double since Nixon and Marcy are both going."

Randy's ears perked up at Marcy's name. "You know, Mom, Harry showed me the brochure on the bus. Maybe I could go too."

"I didn't show you the brochure, jerk," I answered. "You took it."

"Harry, don't say jerk," said Mom.

Randy's eyes drifted to the window that faced Marcy's house. "If I went, I could help keep an eye on him; make sure he doesn't get homesick and all."

"I don't need you to babysit me," I said, frowning. It was so annoying how Randy tried to make himself sound like *Brother of the Year*.

Worst Brother of the Year was more like it.

"I'll discuss it with your father," said Mom as she turned on the stove. "Now get upstairs and start your homework and let me get dinner started." She looked up slyly. "Unless one of you wants to help out…"

"That's okay," we both answered together. That was one thing both Randy and I could agree on.

CHAPTER TWO

D ad said yes to Camp Awonjahela. That's the good news. The bad news was that he said Randy could come too.

A week at camp sounded awesome, but I knew all too well how much tormenting my brother could squeeze into a week when we were out of our parents' view. Would I have even asked to go to camp if I had known Randy would be there too?

Apparently, it helped that Camp Awonjahela has a scholarship program for families with more than one kid. You always hear people say that money isn't the most important thing. I agree, but whoever said that probably also had a lot of money. If we were rich, Dad might not be away working all the time. Then, instead of Camp Awonjahela, we could go camping together at the state park, just him and me. That probably wouldn't work either, since I'm sure Randy would have to come too, but I could dream.

So once Dad said yes, Mom went ahead and registered us for one week at the camp. They gave us a list of everything we needed to bring with us. She sent me to gather my clothes and supplies a week ahead of time so I wouldn't wait until the last minute to pack.

Personally, I think doing things at the last minute is a much more efficient use of time. But Mom says it just creates unnecessary anxiety. Living with Randy, I know all about anxiety, so I decided not to argue with her about it. I try to help her out with things like that when I can. I figure if Randy was my kid, I'd need a break wherever I could get one.

The list said electronics of any kind (including phones, video game players, headphones, and anything like that) were prohibited. That didn't sound fair to me. But Randy would probably have an even harder time managing without electronics for a week. Mom said we'd both have to cope. I guess the camp wants us to get closer to nature and smell the roses. When I thought of that, I reminded Randy to make sure he brought deodorant or else everyone would smell more than the roses, if you know what I mean. He told me to shut up.

I opened my dresser drawer and read the packing list

aloud. "Seven pairs of underwear, seven pairs of socks, swimsuit, extra sneakers, beach towel, bath towel, long pants, sweatshirt." I guess the last two were in case it got cold. "Poncho, shorts, seven t-shirts, toothbrush, toothpaste, shampoo, bar of soap, sunscreen, bug spray, water bottle or canteen, sleeping bag, pillow."

Geesh. That was a lot of stuff. I might have to rent a truck just to carry everything. Later that week, I took the giant duffel bag from the attic and managed to stuff everything in. With my sleeping bag and pillow under one arm and the enormous duffel over the other shoulder, I could barely walk. Randy called me a wimp and said he could carry both of ours no problem, but there was no way I was letting him near my stuff. He'd probably check it into the girls' side of camp or throw it in the lake.

The bus for camp left from the parking lot at the county library. Dad was on another business trip, in Tallahassee this time I think, but he told us over the phone to listen to the counselors and to stay out of poison ivy. He made Randy promise to be nice to me. Randy promised, but I'm pretty sure he had his fingers crossed.

Mom seemed kind of weepy to see us go. She kept giving us instructions even as we waited to board the bus.

"Behave yourselves. And don't forget to brush your teeth. Be careful in the lake. Don't go out too deep.

Harry, try to make some new friends. Randy, don't torment your brother."

It seemed like she was going to repeat everything she'd ever told us before we could leave. Randy finally gave her a hug and stepped on the bus. I felt nervous again. But it was too late to back out now. I gave her one last wave, and then I followed Randy onto the bus.

CHAPTER THREE

The bus to Camp Awonjahela was a lot like the one that took us to school. I sat right next to Nixon. Randy and Marcy were in the back with the older kids. It was a six-hour ride into the mountains to reach camp, but at least we were not going to school. I shuddered at the thought that my schoolteachers might actually be waiting for me at camp, ready to pass out math worksheets. That would be hideous.

Marcy and some of the older girls who had been to camp before were leading the back of the bus in a sing-along. They were singing a silly song about ants marching through the woods. I looked around the rows at the smiling faces and people singing. Mom likes to say that Randy and I are more inventive and play better together when we don't have our electronics to fool with. Maybe that applies to everyone.

"What are you looking forward to most?" asked Nixon.

"I don't know." I thought for a moment. "Maybe the lake?"

Nixon nodded. "Yeah, that will be fun. Marcy says there are lots of games and competitions, too."

"Competitions?" I hadn't heard that. I glanced at Randy in the back of the bus. Most competitions in my house ended up with me in severe pain.

"Yeah," answered Nixon. "The cabins compete against each other in games like tug of war and swimming races. There's even a huge game of capture the flag."

"Cool." Those did sound fun. Maybe if they kept my cabin away from Randy's, the week might be okay.

"Hey!" a shout came from the back of the bus. I turned around to see Marcy stand up quickly and glare at Randy.

I shook my head. Like I said, it was only a matter of time until my brother did something stupid. She marched up the aisle to the front. I don't think you're really supposed to move around like that when the bus is moving, but Mr. Early didn't seem to notice.

Mr. Early was a retired school bus driver who still helped out with driving for summer camps and church groups. He was kind of old. I think Mom raised an eyebrow when she saw he was driving. You'd think with a last name like Early, he'd always be on time, but Mr.

Early was always late. I think that's why he stopped driving kids to school, but Nixon says he got fired.

Marcy sat down in the first row on the right side. She's always super easy to talk to, so not surprisingly, she quickly started chatting with Mr. Early. Nixon told me she volunteers once a month at the Sleepy Pines Nursing Home down the road and reads to the old people who are stuck in their beds. You'd never catch me doing that, but I guess it's pretty nice. Randy was still at the back of the bus talking to Cole Bradley, but he kept staring up front at Marcy.

"Did you know there are three thousand lakes in the Adirondack region of New York State?" said Nixon.

"Uh, huh." I nodded, half listening. Nixon was always coming up with interesting facts like that. Well, at least he thought they were interesting. I think he'd memorized the hundred *National Geographic Fun Fact* books that he'd checked out from the library over the school year. Maybe someday he could be on a game show like *Jeopardy*.

"Yep. There are also three kinds of venomous snakes and more than six thousand black bears."

Bears? I turned and looked him in the eyes. "Really?"

"That's right, and—"

Before Nixon could finish, a shoulder banged into my head from the aisle. "Ouch!" I groaned, looking up.

"Oh, sorry about that, Frog Legs," said Randy, grinning. He continued past our row and sat next to Marcy in the front.

"She's not going to like that," muttered Nixon, watching his sister turn her head toward the window each time Randy tried to talk to her.

I had been asking Nixon for ages if he knew why Marcy put up with Randy in the first place, but he didn't know either. The best we could come up with was she felt sorry for him and liked to help people in need, kind of like the old people in the nursing home. Randy was definitely in need. In need of a new personality.

Marcy still wasn't talking to him, which I knew would make Randy mad. I sunk lower in my seat since when Randy got mad he usually took it out on me. But instead of marching back down the aisle, he stepped into the stairwell by the door of the bus to try and look Marcy in the face.

I know for a fact you're not allowed to stand in the stairwell. Especially when the bus is moving. That's probably even against the law. Maybe if we got pulled over, Randy would be sent to jail.

"Get back to your seat, mister!" Mr. Early yelled. But Randy wasn't listening. He was pleading with Marcy to talk to him, but she kept shaking her head.

"What's he doing?" asked Nixon. "That's not safe."

I nodded in agreement as Mr. Early yelled louder.

"Hey, mister! I said, sit down!" Mr. Early was paying more attention to Randy than he was the road.

Randy finally stepped up out of the stairwell, but he accidentally bumped into the door handle. The front door folded back, a gust of air pouring through the seats. Now everyone was watching. Kids were yelling. The wind was howling. And we were still barreling along the freeway.

Mr. Early lunged to shut the door.

"Watch out!" screamed Marcy.

A tractor-trailer horn blared. The bus had drifted across the lane toward the median and the oncoming traffic!

CHAPTER FOUR

Mr. Early yanked the steering wheel hard to the right. The bus veered so fast, the wheels on its left side rose off the ground. I swear we were on just one set of wheels like some kind of crazy stunt bus. Nixon and I were staring down at the kids on the right side.

Time seemed to stand still. I think I saw my life flash in front of me. Which didn't take very long since I'm only ten, and I don't even remember stuff from when I was a baby.

I caught sight of Randy's face, his eyes bulging in fear. He clung to the front seat for dear life. We were going to die!

The bus hurled across the highway, plowing into a grassy field. A yellow road sign splintered into pieces, flying over the windshield. "Ahh!" everyone screamed. If we'd have been next to a giant cliff, we would have been goners for sure.

"Jumping Jehosaphat!" yelled Mr. Early.

He struggled to straighten the wheel. The bus banged back down onto four wheels. Nixon and I bounced so hard in our seat that I thought our heads were going to smash into the ceiling. Mr. Early slammed on the brakes, and we finally came to a stop in the middle of the field, dirt and dust flying everywhere.

After a moment, the screaming stopped. Everything was eerily quiet. I sat frozen, shocked to be alive.

"Are you okay?" I finally asked Nixon.

He nodded silently.

Cars pulled off the highway and people ran toward us through the field. Mr. Early turned around, his face pale like a ghost.

"Is everyone alright?" His voice was weak and shaky.

Randy was still standing in the aisle. "Get back to your seat!" Mr. Early shouted angrily.

For once, Randy didn't argue. He just nodded and walked quickly down the aisle to the back. Marcy followed him. I might have been imagining things, but I think his eyes looked watery like he was about to cry. Not that I blame him. It must have been terrifying in the stairwell with the door open.

Some grown-ups who had run over from the highway came onto the bus to check on us. No one seemed to have been hurt. We had just been scared out of our minds. The bus still seemed operable, so we slowly drove out of the field to the shoulder of the highway.

As anxious as I'd been about going to camp, I'd never imagined that the ride up would be the most dangerous part.

CHAPTER FIVE

N o one on the bus was singing anymore. I rested my head on the padded seat, listening to the hum of the engine and rhythmic sound of the tires on the pavement. I think Mr. Early was driving ten miles per hour below the speed limit just to be extra careful. I hoped he wouldn't have a heart attack. Mom always says she can't imagine driving a bus full of rowdy kids, and she doesn't know how Mr. Early does it. She'll probably drive me to school in the car for the rest of my life after this.

After a while, the humming sound changed.

"What was that?" asked Nixon.

"It sounded like the engine." I raised my head up over the seat.

"Is that smoke?"

It did look like wisps of smoke were rising from the hood. Mr. Early was shifting into different gears, trying to keep the bus moving normally, it seemed. But the engine was coughing, running rough, and jerking each time he shifted.

"Something's wrong," said Nixon, now stating the obvious. I guess old buses like ours aren't made to go off-roading through grassy fields.

"We gotta make a pit stop, campers," Mr. Early announced over the loudspeaker. Everyone groaned.

The bus turned onto an off-ramp under a big green exit sign. I wondered if we were ever going to get to camp. We sputtered for half a mile down a narrow back road until we reached a service station nestled along the edge of the forest.

We waited while Mr. Early talked to a mechanic. After a few minutes, he came back and told everyone they could get off the bus and stretch their legs while the mechanic checked the engine.

I hoped it wasn't anything serious. If we didn't make it to camp, it would be all Randy's fault. I glared at him in the parking lot, but he looked away. I'm sure he felt bad for causing our bus to nearly crash, but he wasn't going to admit that to me.

Nixon and I went inside the tiny service station to buy a couple candy bars from the vending machine and use the bathroom. When we came out, I noticed the sun was getting low in the sky. The trees behind the service station cast long shadows across the parking lot.

"Do you think they've already done all the fun stuff at camp?" asked Nixon.

"I hope not," I answered. Even though we'd be there for the whole week, it wouldn't be fair if we missed the beginning.

"I wonder what cabin we'll be in?" said Nixon.

"Does it make a difference?"

"I guess not."

That was as interesting as Nixon's and my conversation got as we milled around the parking lot. It seemed like we were there for hours.

A weak cheer rang out when Mr. Early finally announced we could all get back on the bus. He said it was fixed enough for us to make it to camp. That didn't sound super encouraging, but we just wanted to get going. We were all bored, tired, and hungry.

We got moving again on the highway, but before long, the bus started acting up once more. Mr. Early didn't want to stop, but he could only drive thirty miles per hour. So instead of six hours, our ride to camp ended up taking ten.

I wondered if somehow Mom knew about all our problems. I missed not having a phone to communicate with her. This must be how it had felt when Mom and Dad were kids. They always tell us how they never knew what anyone was doing until they reached somewhere.

She told me once that when she grew up they didn't even have the Internet. Weird.

It was really late when we finally turned onto the exit for the camp. Mr. Early drove several miles down a dark, wooded road. I made out the sign over the entrance that said Camp Awonjahela as we parked in front of a large building with a light still on. Half the kids on the bus were sleeping.

"We made it," I said, shaking Nixon who was slouched next to me.

"Everybody off," called Mr. Early.

We groggily trudged out into the night air to pull our bags from the compartment under the bus. We entered the building, which turned out to be the dining hall. A tall man in a baseball hat greeted us at the door, directing us to sit at two of the long tables that stretched across the open rectangular room. The wood paneled walls were decorated with banners and flags, and we passed several boards with lists of names from years and years of summer camps.

"Welcome to Camp Awonjahela, everyone," said the man. "I'm Mike Greenfield, Camp Director. You can call me Mr. G. I'm sorry you had such a tough time getting up here today. We're contacting all your parents to let them know you arrived safely. I promise from here on out we'll have nothing but fun. Sound good?"

There were some mumbled responses between yawns.

It was a big change from the enthusiasm and singing we'd all had when starting the trip. I guess that will happen when your bus nearly crashes and then breaks down on the highway.

"I'm sure you're tired," continued Mr. G, "so let's get you something quick to eat and then off to your cabins for some shut-eye. We have a big day planned tomorrow."

Mr. G and a few other workers brought out packs of small cereal boxes, milk, and bananas to each of the tables. While we ate, he called everyone's name and assigned them a cabin number, first the girls, and then the boys.

Nixon and I were both assigned Cabin Eleven. Randy was in Cabin Six and Marcy was in Cabin Two. I thought I heard a couple older kids chuckle when Mr. G said Cabin Eleven, but I may have been imagining things. At that point, I didn't care where I slept. I was just happy to finally be there.

CHAPTER SIX

T he trail to the boys' cabins wound through the dark woods. We followed Mr. G with our bags like a long, sleepy train behind a locomotive headlight. Above us, millions of stars poked through the treetops, brighter than I'd ever seen them. They didn't look real, more like a painting.

I suddenly felt very far from home. We were in exactly the type of place where all those horror movies are filmed. The kind where some deranged, psycho killer is on the loose and no one is around to hear the victims' screams. Of course, that only happens in stupid movies. I wasn't scared or anything like that, but you know, it did, uh, cross my mind.

We descended a small slope, reaching a clearing where a flagpole stood in the center. Mr. G's light flashed quickly around the edge of the clearing. I caught glimpses of small wooden cabins nestled in the trees. He called out one cabin number at a time and then led the assigned boys up to the door where a counselor met them.

"Good luck with Cabin Eleven, Frog Legs," said Randy as he passed with his friend Cole.

"Why?" I said. "What's wrong with it?"

Randy grinned and disappeared into the darkness.

"What's wrong with Cabin Eleven?" I asked Nixon, but he just shrugged. I think he was still half asleep. I knew Cole had been to the camp before. Did he tell Randy something about our cabin?

Nixon and I were the last two in the courtyard. Mr. G finally came back and walked us up to our door. Each of the cabins was identified with a carved wooden number nailed next to the door. In the shadow from Mr. G's light, it seemed like the "11" had been recently painted. It reminded me of paint patches over graffiti along the highway, but I was too tired to think about it further.

Mr. G rapped lightly and opened the door. A college-aged guy emerged and greeted us. "Ryan will be your counselor for the week, boys," Mr. G said softly. "See you in the morning."

Ryan grunted and waved us past him and into the cabin. His hair was sticking up all over the place, and it looked like he'd been sleeping. We walked into a small rectangular room with bunk beds against three of the walls and a single bed on the fourth. Ryan pointed to one of the bunks and muttered "Goodnight," before collapsing into the single bed.

"I guess this is ours," I whispered to Nixon through the shadows. We stepped over to what I hoped was our empty bunk. "Which one do you want?"

"I'll take the bottom one," Nixon's voice whispered back. "Easier to get to the bathroom."

I'd never slept on a top bunk before, but it sounded good to me. The one time our family had vacationed in Florida, we'd stayed in a condo with bunk beds, but Randy had immediately claimed dibs on the top bunk. Nixon and I unrolled our sleeping bags and pillows and I carefully climbed up the side to the top.

As I lay down on the thin mattress, the bunk creaked so loudly I worried the boards might break. I figured plenty of kids must have slept on it before, so it had to be safe. Then again, maybe they'd all pushed it to the brink of collapsing. I really didn't want to crush Nixon in his sleep. Other than Randy, he was the only guy I knew at camp. Mom always says not to worry about things that are out of your control, though, so I closed my eyes and tried not to think about it.

That's when I heard the noise. It sounded like an animal was clawing at the floorboards or like something terrible was trying to get into the cabin. Maybe it was the psycho killer from the woods.

"What is that?" I whispered down to Nixon.

"I don't know," he replied. "It sounds like...I think someone's snoring."

The sound was getting louder. It was like there was a chainsaw in the middle of the room. I sat up. The noise was coming from Ryan's bed. Unbelievable! How were we going to be able to sleep with that happening all night? I fell back onto the bed, the boards moaning loudly.

"Hey! Be careful!" hissed Nixon from below.

"Sorry."

I suddenly wanted to be back home in my own bed, not stuck out in the woods in the middle of nowhere with a bulldozer. I zipped up my sleeping bag and stuck my pillow over my head. I closed my eyes and wondered if I was ever going to get to sleep.

CHAPTER SEVEN

A shrill sound echoed through the cabin. It was like a fire alarm was right on the other side of the wall. I had no idea what time it was, but it felt like I'd barely closed my eyes. I peered out the window next to my bunk. The sun was up. Someone was standing next to the flagpole playing a trumpet. Several groans filtered around the room and Ryan climbed out of bed in his underwear.

"Rise and shine, maggots," he said, pulling on his clothes. He walked out of the cabin, the door slamming loudly behind him. As annoying as his snoring had been during the night, he seemed to be even worse when he was awake. I wondered why a guy like that would want to be a camp counselor.

A few of the other bunks stirred and a long, high-pitched chirp sounded near the far wall as someone farted. "Aw, James, come on!" a voice called in agony, followed by laughter from the offending bunk.

I sat up and looked around the room. It was even smaller in the light than it had seemed in the dark. I carefully hung my feet over the side of my bed and slid down onto the edge of Nixon's bunk and then onto the floor.

He was still out cold, so I shoved him a bit through his sleeping bag. "Nixon, wake up."

Four other boys were sitting up and getting dressed in the room. "Hey," I said.

"When did you guys get in?" one of them asked.

"I think it was around midnight," I answered, trying to look friendly. "I'm Harry. This is Nixon."

"Hey," said a boy with short, blond hair. "I'm Leo. This is James." He pointed to the brown-haired boy pulling on his glasses in the bottom bunk. "And this is Anthony, and that's Kareem." He pointed to the two boys in the next bunk. "They're twins."

"What's up?" said Kareem. His hair was cut tight against his dark skin. "Where are you guys from?"

"Pennsylvania," I answered. "How about you?"

"Brooklyn," Anthony answered, standing up next to his brother. He was a good three inches shorter than Kareem. His hair was longer and he wore glasses.

"I thought you guys were twins," I said, puzzled.

"Must be fraternal," said Nixon, walking up behind me. "Hey," he said to the other boys.

Kareem chuckled, "This one's smart." He reached out and gave Nixon a fist bump. "What's up?"

Nixon always tells me that the knowledge in his head will come in handy sometime. Maybe it would help us make friends with these guys. Not that my personality couldn't do the trick all by itself of course.

"So, what do we do now?" I asked. Out the window, campers were moving purposefully in and out of the cabins.

Before anyone could answer, Ryan entered the room and waved his hands.

"Okay, come on now, guys. Let's get a move on. Ten minutes until breakfast."

"That," replied Anthony, nodding at Ryan.

"Let's go, ladies!" Ryan called out again, louder. "Double time."

I wondered if Ryan had been in the military or something the way he was barking out orders. Nixon and I turned back to our bunk and straightened our sleeping bags. We quickly changed clothes and followed the other boys down the trail to the bathroom.

Everything looked so different outside in the daylight. Morning sunshine streamed through the huge trees overhead. Kids were buzzing around along the trails. Yesterday's bus ride seemed like it had happened in a different world. Maybe it had been just a bad dream.

The bathroom was better than a Porta-Potty but a lot

worse than what I was used to at home. Two small sinks filled one wall next to the door, opposite a toilet stall and a urinal. A narrow doorway opened to a single shower stall in the back. Two guys blocked the door as we walked in, lined up in the middle of the room for a turn at the sink. They were shoving each other and making faces in the mirror.

When they finished at the sinks, the two guys chuckled at us on their way out the door.

"Cabin Eleven!" they shouted from the trail.

I exchanged looks with Nixon who shrugged again.

"What is that about?" I asked Leo as I bent over the sink to rinse my mouth.

Leo rolled his eyes and spit. "I'll tell you at breakfast."

I was starting to get a bad feeling about our cabin. It wasn't like we were an unlucky number like thirteen. It also couldn't have been anything I'd done. I'd just gotten there. I was pretty sure I hadn't done anything too stupid during the night, but I was pretty tired, so you never knew.

Randy says that one time when he and I were sharing the pullout bed at my grandma's house, I got up in the middle of the night and started playing a tune on her piano. Which is weird because I don't even know how to play the piano.

CHAPTER EIGHT

R yan was already gone when we dropped our toiletries off at the cabin.

"Come on, we can't be late," said Kareem. "Each cabin gets extra points for being on time to meals in the dining hall."

"Is that part of the competition?" asked Nixon.

"Yeah," said Anthony. "And the competition is everything."

"Everything?" I said.

Kareem chuckled. "You'll see."

Most of the long tables were already filled with campers by the time we filed into the dining hall. Numbered signs on small metal stands separated sections of each table by cabin. The girls were on one side of the room, the boys on the other. Ryan and the other counselors seemed to have a table by themselves in the corner.

Leo led our group quickly over to a middle table marked with our cabin number.

"Eleven!" the boys at the section next to us called out and laughed.

I turned to ask Leo to explain what the heck was up with our cabin number, but right then Mr. G started talking over the microphone. He stood on a small stage at the front of the room. There was a projector screen behind him and a narrow podium that looked like it might be used for assemblies.

"Good morning, Camp Awonjahela!"

"Good morning, Mr. G," all the campers sang out in unison.

"Fun, friendship, adventure, and safety!" Mr. G shouted.

"One camp, one memory!" the campers called back.

I raised my eyebrows in surprise at the weird little chant, but no one else seemed to mind.

"It's great to finally have everyone here with us," said Mr. G. "We had some very late visitors from Pennsylvania last night, but we're glad you all made it." He looked around the room and smiled. I was afraid he was going to make us all stand up and recite the chant or take a camp oath, but he didn't.

Leo patted me on the back and grinned. "We were afraid you two weren't coming when you didn't show last night."

"That would have been a disaster for the competition," said Kareem, leaning in from the other side of the table.

"We have to have even numbers in each cabin to make it fair," explained Leo.

"How does the competition work?" I asked.

Leo nodded up at the stage. "Listen, I think he's about to talk about it."

Mr. G had lowered the microphone to talk with one of the other staff members, but now he looked back out at the tables.

"Today is going to be a fantastic day at Camp Awonjahela. Swim tests will be this morning down at Lake Humphrey for the girls' cabins and any remaining boys who were late arriving. The annual tug of war is after lunch, and throughout the rest of the day, we'll be rotating you through some of the group competition categories like archery, rifle range, crafts, outdoor cooking, karaoke, and boating."

Around us kids' faces lit up at the mention of the activities they liked the best. I didn't remember Mom or Nixon describing Camp Awonjahela as a sports camp, but it seemed like there were an awful lot of activities.

"As the week progresses," said Mr. G, "your counselors will keep a tally of your scores. The girls' and boys' cabin with the most points at the end of the week will be our camp champions. Their names will be added to the trophy case of achievement that is over against the wall where Nurse Trella is standing."

He nodded behind us to the doorway. "Give a wave for us, Nurse Trella, so our new campers can see what I'm talking about." An older woman with gray hair waved her arm and smiled next to a wide glass display case.

"You may now send your cabin representative up to get your food trays," said Mr. G. "Enjoy breakfast, and let's make this a great Camp Awonjahela day!"

James sprang up from our table and speed walked to a line of kids forming outside the kitchen. I saw Randy in line ahead of him, chatting with some older kids. For a little while I'd nearly forgotten about my brother being at camp too. Not having him at the forefront of my mind was refreshing, but dangerous. It was never a good idea to get too comfortable with Randy around. That was usually right when he would move in to strike.

"That would be so killer to have our names in there," said Kareem, still staring at the trophy case.

"Give me a break," said a boy from another cabin who was sitting next to us and had overheard Kareem's comment. "Cabin Eleven has never won the competition."

"This week will be different," Kareem replied. "Just watch."

"We'll see." The boy snickered and turned away.

"It's so stupid," said Kareem.

I looked at the rest of the guys, blank-faced. "Okay, what the heck is going on? What's wrong with Cabin Eleven?"

"Yeah," said Nixon, "is it cursed or something?"

"Shh!" the other guys whispered quickly.

"Jeez, dude, don't say that," said Kareem. "What are you trying to do, make things worse?"

"Make what worse?" I asked.

The three of them shared a glance. "They have to know sometime," said Anthony, shrugging.

"I guess you're right," said Leo. He leaned toward Nixon and me. "Not now, though, there's not enough time."

I frowned, wondering what could be so top secret that he couldn't just tell us over breakfast. Leo, Kareem and Anthony had said they'd all been to Camp Awonjahela before, so they knew its traditions. It was probably just some dumb prank the other kids liked to pull. I was used to stuff like that from living with Randy 24/7, so I figured I'd have an advantage.

"Then when?" I asked, staring Leo in the eyes.

"Yeah, we're in the cabin, too," said Nixon. "We have a right to know."

Leo nodded. "Tonight. At the campfire. I'll tell you the whole story."

CHAPTER NINE

J ames arrived back at the table with an enormous tray of pancakes. I slathered my stack with enough syrupy sweetness to drown a small town. Pretty soon I forgot all about hearing the story. Ryan passed out schedules with each of our activities for the day. Nixon and I both had the swim test at the lake first and group activities in the afternoon.

"What do you think the swim test will be?" I asked Nixon, after we changed into our swimsuits. I knew how to swim. I just wasn't ready for the Olympic relay team. All the strokes were confusing—freestyle, breaststroke, and whatever you did for the butterfly.

"I don't think it will be too hard," said Nixon. "Marcy told me you just tread water for a while and then swim laps."

"How many laps?"

"I don't know. Not many." He looked at me suspiciously. "You can tread water, right?"

"Sure." I nodded confidently. And it was true. I could tread water for a little while. I just hoped it wasn't like a movie Randy told me about where they made Navy Seal candidates swim in the pool for seven hours.

We followed a trail along the ridge behind the boys' cabins, passing an intersection with the path to the girls' cabins. At a sign for the lake, we turned down a small hill, joining several groups of girls. I recognized a few guys from our bus too, but the other boys all seemed to have taken their tests the afternoon before while we were broken down on the side of the road.

The trees along the path parted. In front of us was a spectacular, glistening blue lake.

"Wow," said Nixon, as we both stopped and gawked at Lake Humphrey.

"It looks like a postcard," I said.

Between the water and us spread a wide, sandy beach. Several older kids that looked like counselors hit a volleyball back and forth on a sand court. A covered pavilion held picnic benches and had paper streamers draped from the rafters. "Welcome Campers!" was written across a banner hanging along the front. Beyond the beach was a swim area and a floating, wooden dock that extended out into the water in the shape of an "L".

Past the dock was a deeper swim area and a square,

floating platform with a diving board. A shorter dock further up the shore was fitted with canoes and small sail-boats. My only experience on a boat was the time Randy forced me down the river in a canoe. I gulped, remembering how we'd barely survived that trip. I made a mental note to stay clear of the boats as long as possible.

As if on cue, a voice chuckled behind me. "Those are some memories, aren't they, Frog Legs?"

I turned and stared up at my brother's taunting face. I'd forgotten about him again. "Don't get any ideas." I stepped instinctively away. "Come on, Nixon."

We left our towels on a picnic table in the pavilion and joined the line of kids on the dock. Two lifeguards paced along the line, swinging their whistles like they were hot stuff. One of them jumped into the water and swam to the far side of the swim lane.

"Good morning, campers. This is your swim test. In order to swim in the deep end of the lake this week," the first lifeguard said as he pointed out to the roped off area and diving platform, "you'll need to demonstrate that you won't sink to the bottom like a stone. That creates a lot of extra work for us." He smiled at a girl lifeguard who had just walked up like he'd said the funniest thing in the world.

"I think he'd rather work on his tan than rescue anyone," I whispered to Nixon.

"The swim test is simple," said the girl lifeguard,

dropping into the water on the deep side of the dock. "First, you'll need to tread water for one minute without stopping or touching the bottom." She demonstrated treading water as she spoke as if to say it was the easiest thing in the world.

I saw Randy elbow Cole, nodding confidently. I couldn't remember how long I'd actually treaded water before, but one minute didn't seem too long.

"Second," the lifeguard continued, "you'll need to swim one lap across the swim area, from the dock to the far rope and back." She waved to the other lifeguard, who began swimming toward us in fluid strokes. He didn't have goggles or anything, but he swam in a perfectly straight line, popping up right before he hit the dock.

The girl lifeguard, still treading water, smiled and looked up at us. "Any questions?"

"I wonder how deep it is out there," said Nixon, staring at the diving platform.

"Deep enough," a voice next to him answered.

I turned to see a girl with reddish colored hair and a green bathing suit grinning at us.

"What?" I asked, wondering where she came from.

"I said it's deep enough that you won't touch the bottom. At least I never have. But you'll be fine if you know how to swim."

"We can swim," said Nixon.

The girl tilted her head to the side. "He doesn't look

too sure." She pointed her index finger at me like I was some kind of animal on display at the zoo.

I raised my eyebrows, not sure exactly what to say.

"Ivy, come on," said another girl on the dock. She tugged on the girl in the green bathing suit's arm.

"Don't sink!" the girl named Ivy called to us as she skipped over to her friends.

"She's weird," said Nixon as the line started moving forward.

"Yeah," I said, watching her talk to her friends across the dock. As I was staring at Ivy, I was startled by a yell from right behind me.

"Feel the breeze, boys!" Randy and Cole had snuck up behind us. I watched in terror as Cole yanked Nixon's bathing suit down to his ankles. Thankfully Nixon was wearing underwear beneath his suit.

Then I felt Randy's hands tugging at my waist. My heart nearly stopped as I remembered I was not wearing anything beneath my suit. Mom had specifically reminded me to conserve my socks and underwear so I made it through to the end of the week. My brain fast-forwarded. I imagined the humiliation of standing naked in front of the entire swim area full of girls.

I'm not sure what happened next. Maybe a shot of adrenaline coursed through my body. My science teacher, Mr. Carmichael, says that can happen when we're in mortal danger. Or maybe it was just instinct, a result of living with Randy.

"No!" I screamed, twisting violently in Randy's grasp. We wrestled to the edge of the dock. My foot slipped off the edge. We both tumbled into the water.

It was shallow enough to stand. I wiped the water from my eyes, only to see everyone pointing and laughing hysterically. Randy was grinning from ear to ear. He held my swimsuit in his hand, hoisted over his head like a trophy.

I don't think anyone could see anything, but I quickly sunk lower in the dark water. I shot Randy a hateful stare as the lifeguard took the suit and tossed it to me.

"I think you failed the test, Harry!" Randy roared, as Cole pulled him back up onto the dock.

I saw Nixon step deeper into the crowd, shaking his head. Ivy stood with her friends, her hand over her mouth in surprise.

It was terrible.

CHAPTER TEN

Maybe it was my imagination, but everybody seemed to snicker when they walked past me after my brother's stupid prank. The swim test turned out to be a piece of cake. I had no problem treading water and one lap across the swim area wasn't very far. The lifeguards didn't even care what kind of stroke we used.

Nixon and I swam for a little while after the test, but we kept a careful distance from Randy and his friends. I knew going to camp with Randy was a bad idea. Mom always says you can't teach an old dog new tricks. I think it's the same thing with older brothers. If they're a jerk to you at home, they'll probably act that way at camp too.

Nixon and I dried off under the pavilion, and then went back to the cabin to change. We met up with the rest of the cabin at the craft tent, but we didn't say anything about what happened on the docks. I figured word would probably get out eventually, but who knows, maybe I'd get lucky and people would forget about it.

Leo, Kareem, James, and Anthony were each finishing their second project, making a birdhouse out of graham crackers and pretzels. I wasn't sure how long that would hold up outside, but Jackie, the counselor who was directing crafts, said it was an edible house. Leo showed me how the houses fit together and I made one pretty quickly as they finished up. He said that the crafts didn't officially count as one of the categories in the competition, but it was good practice working together. Even though we'd missed half of it, I did feel like I was getting to know the other guys a little bit more.

At lunch, it was my turn to be the waiter for our table, so I filed into the line outside the kitchen. It was similar to the lunch line at school, except no one was complaining about the food.

"Where's the bug juice?" asked James, when I finally sat down to eat.

"Harry didn't get it," said Kareem.

"What kind of juice?" I asked, wondering what I'd missed. There were silver pitchers of water already on the tables.

"Bug juice, man," said Anthony. "It's the best juice in the world."

"Over there," explained Leo, pointing to the far side of the kitchen.

I hurried over and grabbed the last remaining plastic pitcher. I set it down in front of the guys at the table.

"Bug juice!" they yelled in unison.

Nixon looked curious as he poured the red liquid into his paper cup. "Why do they call it bug juice?"

"Because it's made of bug blood, of course," said Anthony, laughing.

Nixon's face turned pale as he lowered the cup away from his mouth. The other guys cracked up as they poured themselves refills.

"I think they're kidding, Nixon." I tried a sip and realized it was like fruit punch.

"Right," Nixon said sheepishly. "I knew that."

I felt a little bad for him after what had happened at the lake, even though I got the worst of it. Randy was my brother, but Nixon caught a lot of collateral damage by being my friend. His nerves were probably frayed.

During lunch, every cabin assigned a representative to lead each event in the competition. I got the overnight hike. I didn't know anything about hiking. I've certainly never camped out overnight in the woods.

Leo must have noticed my wary expression. "It'll be fun," he said. "This is the first year we actually get to camp out overnight. Last year our age group just day hiked and then slept back in our cabin. I've been looking forward to it all year. That and Ultimate."

"What's Ultimate?"

He smiled. "The final competition on the last night—
Ultimate Capture the Flag."

"What makes it Ultimate?" I asked. I'd played regular
Capture the Flag in gym class, but I had never heard it
called Ultimate.

"It covers the entire camp property and is worth the
most points of all the competitions. It's epic. And don't
worry. Being the captain for an activity isn't a big deal.
Most activities are performed by everyone."

As we waited to finish up lunch, Ivy, the girl from the
lake, walked over. "Sorry about this morning," she said,
smiling. "I'm glad you didn't drown."

I felt my face turning red as she walked away.

"Harry, did you just talk to Poison Ivy?" asked Leo,
his eyebrows raised.

"Uh, I guess so," I mumbled. I wasn't sure why she
kept talking to me. I didn't really know what the big deal
was, but I wasn't going to lie about it. Mom always says
that you should try to be friendly with everyone even if
you don't want to spend all day with them.

"We met her at the swim test," said Nixon. I glared at
him, but he didn't get the hint and kept talking. "She was
worried Harry would drown."

The guys all snickered, and I thought I saw James say
"pantsed" to Anthony and laugh.

"Dude, you need to watch out for her," said Kareem.
"She's trouble. That's why everyone calls her Poison Ivy."

I shrugged. "She seemed nice."

"Oh no, guys," said Anthony, laughing harder. "Harry's got a crush on Poison Ivy. He's definitely a goner."

"I do not. I don't even know her." I glanced at the girls' side of the room without thinking. Ivy was sitting at the Cabin Three table and talking with some other girls. Somehow she caught my stare from all the way across the room and gave a big wave. I snapped back around and stared down into my bug juice. All the guys laughed.

"What's the next activity?" I whispered to Nixon.

"What?"

I gritted my teeth. "What's the next activity?"

"Our karaoke competition starts in ten minutes at the Rec Center," Nixon answered.

I stood up and turned to the exit. I wasn't anxious to sing, but I needed air. "I've gotta go to the bathroom. I'll meet you guys over there."

"Aw, come on, Harry, we're just joking," said Leo. "Don't be mad."

I nodded and tried to smile. "Right. I'll meet you there."

CHAPTER ELEVEN

The karaoke competition was fun. Well, more fun than I'd expected, at least. We were matched up against Cabin Nine, a group of six guys the same age as us. Most importantly, Randy and his goons weren't there. It was a relief not to be constantly looking over my shoulder.

I'm not a great singer, but I was paired with Leo, and we did a song about some guy's sweet home in Alabama. We cracked up the whole time but managed to get through it. Mom says it's good for everybody to try new things and step out of their comfort zone sometimes, which is pretty much what I did.

Each group picked one camper to sing in the finals. The ranking at that performance would count as the points for the competition. We chose James, which surprised me since he seemed kind of quiet like Nixon.

He turned out to be great. He said his mom is a music teacher and his sister sings the national anthem before lots of minor league baseball games where he lives in New Jersey.

You just never know what someone's secret talent might be. I'm not sure what doing karaoke will get you in life, but I guess it's something. We ended up with one more competition point than Cabin Nine, and it felt great to get an early win.

After karaoke, all the boys' cabins met on the beach for a ropes competition. The first part was rope climbing. Two boys from each cabin had to race to the top of a rope tied to a tree branch thirty feet off the ground. I didn't try that part, but Kareem and Anthony said they climbed ropes in gym class back home all the time, so they were our competitors. The counselor who was judging said he would use a graduated scoring system to give a time allowance for the younger kids, so Kareem and Anthony came in third overall.

Finally, we lined up in the sand in front of the pavilion next to a long, woven rope for tug of war. The cabins were split into two teams. Randy was on our team, which kept him from trying to do anything treacherous. He's pretty strong, so it didn't hurt to have him pulling for us either. The contest was best out of three, and while we lost the first round, our team came back and won the final two. All the cabins on the winning side were awarded two cabin points.

After the rope competition, the girls' cabins joined us for free time at the lake until dinner. I was going to swim out to the diving platform, but Randy and all his friends were out there goofing off to impress the girls, so I stayed away.

I thought I saw Ivy looking in my direction a couple times, but thankfully she didn't try to talk to me. I didn't know exactly why kids called her Poison Ivy, but I wasn't going to chance any more embarrassment. I had enough to worry about with Randy. The guys in my cabin seemed pretty cool so far, but I didn't want to give them any more openings to tease me.

At dinner, Mr. G updated everyone on the cabin competition scores. It was hard to know what the totals would be since being on time for meals and other activities also added to the scores in addition to the events. Not surprisingly, Randy's Cabin Six was leading the boys with ten points. Next was Cabin Eight, another group of middle schoolers, with nine points. We were tied for third with Cabin Nine with six points. Cabin Ten only had four points, but they were even younger than us.

The guys weren't happy about being tied for second to last, but with only five cabins, I didn't think it was too bad. Sometimes just finishing is the important thing. Not being last is something to be proud of. Sure, I wanted to win, but you have to be realistic too. My teacher once told me I have a lot of untapped potential. I think that means I have an opportunity to do big things, but I'm smart enough to know my limits. If I could survive the week with Randy and avoid total humiliation, I'd be a winner in my book.

In cabin time after dinner, Ryan made us clean our bunks and get everything in tiptop shape. He said Mr. G would be making surprise inspections throughout the week. Any cabin that was not up to cleanliness standards would lose a point. Leo complained that the campers from the previous week had left things in a big mess so there was more for us to clean up, but Ryan didn't buy it.

We couldn't afford to lose any points, so we all took the cleaning seriously. When we finished, I think even my mom would have been impressed by how the place looked, and she's a real stickler for cleanliness.

CHAPTER TWELVE

The sun had sunk behind the pines that stretched high around the camp, penning us in like the giant walls of a fort. Our cabin gathered around a bonfire at the small amphitheater built into a clearing near the beach. Ryan brought ingredients for Smores from the dining hall. After we'd sufficiently burned our marshmallows on flaming sticks, we stuffed them onto our graham crackers and chocolate squares for a delicious, but messy, treat.

As the fire burned low, Ryan wandered off with some of the other counselors. We sat alone on log seats by the fire at the edge of the woods. I realized it was my chance to get to the bottom of all the Cabin Eleven business.

Leo leaned forward, the light from the fire illuminating his face in the darkness. He stared at me solemnly, like he was about to reveal classified government secrets.

The noises of the forest echoed around us. I didn't think he was ever going to begin, but finally he spoke.

"Camp Awonjahela first opened in 1967."

"It was 1969," said Kareem.

"Quiet," said Leo. "Don't interrupt me."

"You said '67, it was '69," repeated Kareem.

"It doesn't matter. I'm telling this story." Leo shook his head impatiently. "So back in 1967," he paused and stared coldly at Kareem, "or '69, whichever it was…"

Kareem nodded proudly as Leo kept talking. "There were only ten cabins. Five for the boys and five for the girls. As you've probably seen, the girls' are on the other side of the dining hall in their own courtyard. Their cabins numbered one through five. The boys' cabins were numbers six through ten."

"Then how are we Cabin Eleven?" asked Nixon.

Leo glared at him.

"Sorry," said Nixon.

"Keep going," urged Anthony.

"In the first year of the camp, toward the very end of the summer, two of the kids in Cabin Seven were playing with matches. Now I don't know if they were sneaking a smoke, or if they were just a couple of little pyros, but they were burning something in the cabin."

"Trace Parker," said Kareem.

"Right, Trace Parker and Eddie Smith," Leo sighed. "Now keep in mind, this was back in the sixties. Just about everybody smoked, so there were probably matches and lighters all over the place."

"It wasn't as widely known then that cigarette smoke causes lung cancer," said Nixon.

Leo nodded. "Right. But before long, whatever Trace and Eddie were doing had caused the curtains to catch fire. Soon the whole place was ablaze."

"I don't remember any curtains in the cabins," I said, thinking back to when I looked out the window at the trumpet player.

Anthony raised his eyebrows. "Exactly. They took them out of all the cabins after the fire."

"Oh," I said. "So what happened? Were they okay?"

"Well, the whole cabin was burning. The windows and doors were all closed. Smoke was everywhere."

"That was stupid," said Nixon.

"Yes, it was," said Leo. "The camp director back then was a guy named Jeremiah Potterfield."

"What kind of name is that?" Nixon asked, saying the same thing I was thinking.

"I don't know," said Leo, "but he was a young guy who'd just returned from the war."

"World War Two?" asked James.

"Vietnam," said Kareem.

Leo nodded. "He was walking through the courtyard on his way to the lake when he saw the smoke pouring from the burning roof. He didn't know whether there were any kids in there, but he ran in to check. He found poor Trace Parker lying unconscious on the floor, overcome by the smoke. Jeremiah didn't hesitate. He jumped through the flames, picked Trace up, and carried him out of the cabin. As he went back to check for anyone else, the roof collapsed. He was trapped under a beam in the doorway."

I stared into the flames of the bonfire. I couldn't help but picture the cabin burning with Potterfield and the camper trapped inside. "What happened?"

"Well, poor Jeremiah Potterfield was stuck under the beam, but some other people had seen the smoke by this point. They rushed over and pulled him from the flames. They saved his life, but his leg was crushed. The entire right side of his body was badly burned."

I looked back at Leo and then at the other guys. Was he just telling a tall tale? They all seemed serious. Maybe it *was* true.

"What about the other kid?" I asked.

"Yeah, Eddie Smith," said Nixon.

"He died," blurted out Kareem.

"In the fire," said Anthony.

"Of course it was in the fire, stupid," said Kareem.

"They never got him out?" asked Nixon.

"They didn't find his body until the whole cabin had burned to the ground. No one knew he'd been there. Trace Parker was too injured to tell." Leo lowered his voice solemnly. "When they searched through the rubble, they found his charred remains and the metal from his half-melted glasses."

I closed my eyes. I didn't want think about such a terrible thing happening. The Camp Awonjahela brochure hadn't said anything about a fire or deaths. I guess it wasn't the kind of thing a camp would advertise, especially since it had been nearly fifty years ago.

"So what's that have to do with our cabin?" asked Nixon. "Where did Cabin Eleven come from if there were only ten cabins?"

"Exactly," said Leo. "There *were* only ten cabins. But when number seven burned down and Eddie died, they didn't just rebuild it in the same place. They planted six red maple trees there in his memory instead. A new cabin was constructed over on the other side of ten."

"Cabin Eleven," Nixon muttered.

"So what's the problem?" I asked. Sure, our cabin was a replacement for the one that had burned down, but it wasn't in the same place. It wasn't even the same number. There was nothing wrong with it.

"You haven't heard the worst part yet," said Anthony, leaning in.

"Worst?" I raised my eyebrows. "How could anything be worse than a cabin burning to the ground with a kid inside, nearly killing two other people?"

"Well, judge for yourself," said Leo, "but if you're

going to be at Camp Awonjahela, you're going to want to know about this part."

"Especially if you're in Cabin Eleven," added Kareem.

"What is it?" whispered Nixon. I was worried he was going to have a heart attack. I noticed my palms were sweating too, but maybe it was just the heat from the fire.

"Well, there're a lot of superstitious people out there," Leo explained. "Legend has it that after Eddie Smith died, his spirit stayed at Camp Awonjahela."

"Sometimes," said Kareem, "people say you can hear Eddie's voice. It calls to you through those red maples they planted over the ashes of Cabin Seven. And if you're really quiet, they say you can hear his footsteps creaking on the floorboards in Cabin Eleven, still trying to find an escape from the fire."

I realized I wasn't breathing and tried to force myself to exhale. "That's not true," I said. "Who told you all this?"

"I know, it sounds crazy," Leo admitted, "but my older brother has been coming here for years. He's in college now, but he told me all about it before I came last year."

"It's common knowledge," said Kareem.

Nixon looked scared out of his wits. "I think I heard something last night!"

"That was Ryan snoring," I said, shaking my head.

Nixon was my best friend and all, but sometimes he was way too gullible.

"Maybe it was, maybe it wasn't," said Leo. "Jeremiah Potterfield survived the fire, but like I said, his leg was crushed and he was badly burned. It was a long time before he came back from the hospital in Albany. As Camp Director, he had a house on the other side of the lake where he lived year-round. After he got out of the hospital, he holed up over there to recover."

"And he still lives there," said Kareem in an eerie whisper.

"Still? He's not dead by now?" I tried to do some quick math in my head. If the guy was in his twenties in 1969, that was almost fifty years ago. That would make him in his seventies. I guess that was possible. But he'd be an old man.

"He stays in his house on the other side of the lake," said Leo. "No one sees him much. But he has been here. Outside the cabins. Limping along. Staring into the trees."

"What was he doing?" I asked, my heart pounding. I tried not to think about waking up in the middle of the night and seeing a creepy, deformed old man staring at me.

"I don't know," answered Leo. "But my brother said one time they found him inside Cabin Eleven. He was standing there in the middle of the room, staring at the kids sleeping."

"Freaky, right?" asked Anthony, a grin on his face.

"Totally," said Nixon softly.

I didn't know if I believed that part. I didn't know if I believed any of it. Summer camp was supposed to be my break. I already wasn't getting away from being picked on by Randy. I didn't want to have to worry about a curse or some burned psycho too.

"So now nobody likes the kids in Cabin Eleven?" asked Nixon.

"It's not that they don't like us," said Kareem. "They just think it's unlucky for us to be in there."

"It's cursed," said James blankly.

I gulped as I looked at the faces around the fire. No one was laughing. They seemed to believe it, even if they didn't want to.

CHAPTER THIRTEEN

My mind was racing so fast with thoughts about Leo's story that I barely noticed the rustling sound. I stared into the crackling fire. But then the bushes in the shadows behind Kareem's bench began to shake.

Was it the spirit of Eddie Smith? Jeremiah Potterfield wandering the woods?

"Uh, guys," I said, standing slowly. "What was that?"

Everyone turned in the direction I was looking. "What is it?" asked Leo.

"Listen." I stared into the darkness. Was it only my imagination?

"It's just the wind, man," said Anthony.

"I think it's time to go back," said Nixon.

But before anyone could move, the campfire exploded.

BANG! BANG! BANG!

Popping and crackling sounded everywhere.

"Get down!" screamed Leo.

We all dropped to the ground with our hands over our heads. It was like we were under attack.

"What the heck was that?" exclaimed Kareem when the popping sound stopped.

I opened my eyes, half-expecting to see the woods on fire. The air smelled like sulfur. A thick smoke hovered over the fire. I heard laughter from the bushes behind us.

"Oh, no," I groaned.

"Who's there?" called Kareem.

Randy and Cole emerged from the underbrush, laughing their butts off. A half-empty pack of firecrackers was in Cole's hands.

"It's just my stupid brother, guys," I said, shaking my head.

"You should have seen your face, Frog Legs," cackled Randy. "You thought you were a goner!"

"Don't call me that," I shouted. Being teased at home was bad enough. I didn't want my new friends to think I was a loser.

"How long have you been back there?" asked Leo.

"Long enough," said Randy. "That's quite a story you're telling."

"Yeah, did you pee your pants?" asked Cole. "That's all just an old legend, you know."

"The truth is they just put all the losers in Cabin Eleven," said Randy. "You're the only curse."

"Firecrackers aren't allowed at camp, you know," said James. "We could tell Mr. G."

Cole scowled at us. "Oh, I've got a lot more than firecrackers, kid." He picked up a stick from the edge of the bonfire. He took a step toward us, waving the flames back and forth through the air. "But you're not going to tell anyone about that, now, are you?"

I opened my eyes wide. I knew Randy was mean, but maybe Cole was just plain crazy. I didn't want to stick around and find out.

"Let's get out of here, guys," Leo said, turning toward the trail.

"Yeah, that's what I thought," jeered Cole. He threw the stick back into the fire. Sparks flew up into the darkness.

"Do you think he really has more than firecrackers?" asked James, as we walked up the trail to the cabin.

"Don't worry about it, James," said Kareem. "Guys like that are all talk."

"Sorry about that," I said, walking next to Leo. "Randy's a creep."

Leo nodded. "Don't worry about it. I have an older brother in college, remember?"

"Does he bully you too?"

"Sometimes. But he's not around much anymore.

Now I actually miss him, believe it or not. Does Randy always call you that name?"

I shrugged. "Pretty much."

"That sucks."

"Yeah."

"Well…" said Anthony, turning around in front of us. "You did choose to come to the same camp as him."

I laughed. "Right. What was I thinking?"

"And it's not like you're in the most cursed cabin in the history of summer camps," said Kareem.

"Oh, no," I said, laughing harder. "Nothing like that." I was glad the guys had a sense of humor. I didn't have a lot of friends at home besides Nixon. Mom always says that people are safer in numbers. Or was it that misery loves company? Either way, it was nice to have new friends.

Anthony was the first one into the cabin. "What the heck!" he yelled as we ran to catch up.

"Oh, no," said Leo.

I stepped through the doorway and scanned the room. It was completely trashed. All the mattresses were pulled off the bunks. Everyone's bags were dumped.

"Who did this?" demanded Kareem, seething with anger.

"We'd just cleaned everything up," said Anthony. "We'll never pass inspection like this."

I closed my eyes, praying I hadn't brought further misfortune down on my new friends.

"Did you see this?" called James from outside on the steps. We leaned out the door to see him pointing at the side of the cabin. Someone had spray painted a red circle with a line through it around the number eleven. We'd all charged in so quickly we hadn't noticed it.

"Maybe this cabin *is* cursed," said Nixon.

"It doesn't matter," said Leo. "We'll get through it. There's only one way to show whoever did this that they're wrong." He turned to Kareem.

"That's right," said Kareem. "The competition."

"The competition?" Nixon repeated. "What about it?"

"We have to win," said Kareem.

"Is that even possible?" I asked. It seemed unlikely we could beat the older kids. Especially with everyone against us.

Leo grinned. He lifted a corner of my mattress toward the top bunk and helped me push it into place. "Anything's possible, Harry. You just have to believe."

I frowned. It was hard to feel positive right then. I felt like I was back home in my war zone. I pulled my sleeping bag off the floor, spreading it flat over the mattress. A lump inside suddenly moved. I leaped backward, nearly toppling over Nixon.

"What's wrong?" he asked.

I pointed to the sleeping bag. "Something moved."

"Maybe it's Poison Ivy," laughed Kareem. "You didn't bring her back to the cabin, did you, Harry?"

"What is it?" asked Anthony as everyone gathered around my bunk.

"I don't know." I was afraid to touch it again. Maybe it was a poisonous snake. How many different varieties had Nixon said were in the mountains?

"Do you want me to open it?" asked Kareem.

I shook my head and swallowed hard. I didn't want to look like a bigger wimp in front of the guys than I already did. It was my sleeping bag. If anyone was going to open it, it was going to be me.

I climbed the bunk and slowly pulled the zipper open as far as I could reach. In one motion, I flung the top of the bag toward the wall and leaped off the ladder. As I jumped, something landed on my shoulder.

"Ahh!" I screamed, the guys scrambling out of my way.

Then Kareem started cracking up. I turned to see a green bullfrog squatting next to me on the wooden floor.

"Ribbit!" it croaked loudly.

I shook my head, silently cursing my brother. I brushed myself off, then carried the frog to the door.

"Don't hurt it," said Nixon.

"Yeah, it's not the frog's fault," said James.

I dropped the frog gently outside the door. The others

were still laughing, but Leo put his arm around my shoulder. "Relax, Harry. It's funny."

"At least we know who trashed the cabin," said Kareem.

I groaned, picturing Randy's face.

"And I stand by what I said before," said Leo, turning to the group.

"What's that?" I asked.

"The best revenge is to win the competition," Leo replied. "There's nothing Randy can do to take that away from us."

"Yeah," said Kareem. "We'll show them there's no curse."

I knew they were probably right. Standing up for myself was usually the only thing that worked back home with Randy. Maybe winning the competition would prove that Cabin Eleven wasn't unlucky and make him leave us alone.

"What do you think?" asked Leo.

"Let's do it," said Nixon.

James stepped forward. He spit into his hand before holding it out to me.

I raised my eyebrows. "What is that?"

"Spit-shake on it," said James, his face serious.

"Is that even a real thing?" I asked.

Leo grinned then spit into his hand too. "Cabin Eleven." He held it out to James and they shook wildly.

Before I knew it, everybody in the cabin was spitting and shaking. It was crazy. I guess it was peer pressure, but I gathered saliva in my mouth and spit in my hand. I shook with each of the others, one at a time.

"Cabin Eleven!" everyone chanted loudly.

It's weird, but I felt a lot better after that. It was like I wasn't fighting against Randy all by myself. I had friends behind me, and not just Nixon. Cabin Eleven had each other's backs, and I wondered if maybe, just maybe, we might actually be able to pull this off.

"I'm going to go wash my hands now, man," laughed Kareem. "That was kind of disgusting."

CHAPTER FOURTEEN

In the morning, after breakfast, we marched to the rifle and archery range located on the other side of the girls' cabins. We were greeted by Chuck, a staff member who looked older than Ryan and the other counselors. That seemed wise, considering that guns and bows and arrows were dangerous.

The rifle range reminded me of the golf ball driving range next to our grocery store. It was an open building covered by a wooden roof. Half a dozen spots were marked off with carpet mats. About twenty-five yards out from the building was a long, wooden wall. Paper targets were tacked up across from each shooting mat. Warning signs and yellow caution tape was everywhere to ensure no one wandered behind the target wall.

I had never shot a gun or an arrow in my life, unless you counted the Nerf guns that Nixon and I fired at each other in our backyards. I was pretty good at that. I liked to hide in Nixon's tree house and sneak attack him when he walked underneath.

Of course, that was just pretend, and I'd never want to shoot anybody for real. Mom is always telling us to remember that Nerf guns are different than real guns. I think she knows I can tell the difference, but she says it's part of her job as a responsible parent to talk about it.

I know lots of people in my town like to hunt. I guess that's fine, but we don't have any real guns in our house. Randy told me his friend Max once showed him his dad's hunting rifle. My eyes had opened wide thinking about Randy being anywhere near a hunting rifle without a grown-up. I'd like to think that even Randy knows better than to fool around with guns, but I wouldn't bet on it.

We each sat on a carpet square as Chuck unlocked a cabinet. He pulled out six brown rifles, which he called .22's. Then, from a separate locked carrying box, Chuck removed several boxes of ammunition. He gave us protective glasses and foam earplugs then talked about safety. He told us to treat a gun as if it were always loaded, to only point it in a safe direction downrange toward the targets, and to never walk onto the range until the all-clear signal. Stuff like that.

Chuck demonstrated how to lie on our stomachs on the carpet in the prone position, how to load a round into the gun, how to hold it steady on the wooden blocks at the front of our station, and how to use the sight to line up the target. There was a loud pop when he fired a shot at the wooden fence, followed by the ping of a metal plate behind the target. It wasn't as loud as I thought it might be, but I still jumped. I could just make out a mark near the middle of the bullseye on Chuck's target.

"Nice shot!" said Leo.

"It takes some practice," Chuck explained, "but give it a try. I guarantee you'll get better if you work at it." He handed us each a gun and a box of ammunition. We would have time to practice before a shoot-off that would count for our cabin's score in the competition.

"What do you think?" I asked Nixon as we stretched out on our carpets next to each other.

"Doesn't look too hard."

I nodded and carefully loaded a bullet into the gun as Chuck had taught us. I tried to look like I knew what I was doing. The rifle felt heavy in my hands. I set it slowly on the wood block in front of us, stretching my elbow out to the side for support. I closed one eye and stared down the barrel through the sight guide.

I focused on the target. It seemed far away. I tried to block out the other guns firing. Take the safety off. Exhale. My finger inched back against the metal trigger.

Bang!

The gun popped quickly, surprising me as the resistance on the trigger gave way. I felt a surge of excitement as I raised my head to look at my target. I frowned, not seeing a mark.

"I think you missed it," Nixon said, chuckling next to me.

"How?" I asked suspiciously. "I lined it up in the sights like he showed us." I decided to watch Nixon fire one to see if I was doing something wrong. "Let's see you do it any better."

He lined his eye up to the sight. "Okay. Watch this."

I moved my eyes to his target as he fired the gun with a pop. Ping! A hole appeared on one of the outer rings of the paper target.

"Yes!" Nixon said, a smile curling across his lips.

I frowned and bent back over my gun. "Lucky shot."

It took me a dozen tries to get my aim right, but once I figured out how to use the sights correctly, I started hitting the paper on most shots. I didn't get too many in the middle of the bullseye, but at least I was hitting something. It was fun to feel like a real marksman. I pictured myself living back in the old west, riding a horse and carrying a rifle.

When it came time for the shoot-off, Nixon and Anthony were our best shots. Chuck recorded their scores for the competition.

The archery range was even more fun than the rifles. It was set up in the opposite direction to the rifle range, with wide, circular targets mounted on bales of hay.

Chuck said I had a natural form. In the finals, Leo and I had the best scores, so they counted for the competition.

I was happy to be able to contribute something to help our team. We didn't know yet how we'd match up against the other cabins, but Chuck said we'd done well. From what he'd seen so far, he thought we'd likely finish in the top three.

CHAPTER FIFTEEN

After lunch, Mr. G held a surprise inspection of the cabin. He said we were in tiptop shape, despite Anthony leaving a dirty sock under his bunk. He gave us our full competition credit, but he also warned that there could be another inspection later in the week.

"Who's captain for the overnight?" asked Mr. G after he'd finished the inspection.

I reluctantly raised my hand.

"Come with me."

I followed Mr. G outside the cabin. Six empty blue hiking backpacks were lined up next to a tree. He picked up three and I grabbed the others. We brought them inside and handed them out.

"Each of your packs will weigh approximately twenty-five pounds when you've added your gear and supplies," Mr. G explained.

Kareem smirked. "That's easy."

Mr. G smiled. "It might seem like nothing, but I assure you that after a couple hours hiking with twenty-five pounds on your back, you'll be plenty tired."

"Why does it weigh twenty-five pounds?" asked James. "Are there bricks in it or something?"

"Just yours, James," said Leo, sarcastically.

Mr. G chuckled and picked up my pack. "This isn't the kind of camping you might have done with your families. We won't drive up to the campsite with all your supplies. There are no giant tents or twenty-gallon coolers filled with ice. We've stocked the site with firewood, but everything else will be carried in on your backs. Clothes, sleeping bag, food, cooking supplies, toilet paper—"

"Kareem can carry the toilet paper," joked Anthony.

"How far away is the campsite?" I asked, picturing hours of hiking up a mountain.

Mr. G handed my pack back. "It's three miles to the site. We'll get a fire going, make dinner, sing some songs, maybe perform a few skits, and then get some sleep. My guess is everyone will be pretty tired by that time."

"And then the helicopters come and fly us out in the morning, right?" asked Leo, grinning.

Mr. G laughed. "Not this time, Leo. But I'll keep that in mind for next year." He turned to the doorway. "Ryan, do you have these boys ready for lake events this afternoon?"

Ryan nodded, staring down at his clipboard. "Wouldn't miss it," he said dryly. He'd been mostly quiet during Mr. G's visit. He seemed to prefer spending his time with the other counselors and probably didn't want to give away that he barely knew us.

Mr. G gave Ryan a skeptical glance, but then smiled at us. "It's one of my favorites. Paddle hard boys, and good luck." He motioned for Ryan to follow him to the courtyard.

"What events are at the lake?" asked Nixon, once Mr. G and Ryan had left.

"Canoeing, sailing, and swimming," said Leo. "We can pick two people for each event."

"I call dibs on swimming," said Kareem quickly.

"Me too," said Anthony. "We both rock in the water."

"We're Water Moccasins," said Kareem. "That's the name of our swim team at the Brooklyn Y."

"They're venomous," said Nixon.

"That's right," said Kareem, smiling. "We're dangerous in the water."

"Okay, you guys can swim," said Leo. "I know how to sail. Does anyone else?" When everyone shook their heads, he turned to me. "Harry, you look like a sailor."

I raised my eyebrows. Randy had said I looked like a lot of things over the years, most of them not nice, but sailor had never been one of them.

"I do *not* know how to sail."

"It's easy," said Leo. "I'll teach you."

"I don't think that's a good idea," I said.

"Would you rather paddle the canoe?"

I remembered the time Randy had almost killed me on a canoe and was about to object, but Nixon beat me to it.

"I'll canoe," Nixon volunteered.

"Me too," said James.

Leo looked back and me and shrugged. "Looks like you're sailing, Harry."

Leo sounded like he knew what he was doing. What's the worst that could happen?

Ryan walked back into the cabin and began barking out orders. "Okay, you heard him. Grab your suits and towels and get down to the lake. I'll meet you there." He turned and looked at Nixon and me with a smirk. "And try to hold on to your shorts this time, you two."

A few of the guys chuckled. I could tell they'd heard about Randy's stupid prank on the docks. I tried to ignore it as I got ready for the lake, but I wore two layers this time, just to be safe.

CHAPTER SIXTEEN

Most of the other cabins were already there when we reached the lake. Counselors were taking names of who was competing in each event. Lines formed on the dock for swim races. Canoes were perched on the edge of the sand next to three brightly colored sailboats. Everyone was buzzing with energy around the water.

I was already sweating in the hot sun. It was supposed to be the warmest day of the week, and I suddenly envied Kareem and Anthony for getting to swim. I looked forward to getting the boating race over with. Ryan had told us we'd have free swim after the events and I couldn't wait to relax in the refreshing water.

We walked over to a tall sign hanging from the roof of the pavilion. It listed the current standings in the cabin competition.

"We need to take at least third in lake events to even have a shot at winning," said Leo, staring at the results.

"We've got swimming covered," said Kareem.

"Yeah, you told us, Water Moccasin," Leo replied.

Cabin Eleven was still in fourth place. Randy's cabin was in first, but Cabin Eight was only one point behind. I looked around for my brother and spotted him standing in the line for the canoe race. At least I wouldn't have to go up against him.

Swimming was first and, as promised, Kareem and Anthony both swam strong. Each race was four laps across the swim area. Kareem finished first, and Anthony came in second. In the canoe race, Randy dominated. He and another guy in his cabin came in first place by a wide margin. James and Nixon finished third behind Cabin Eight. Nixon was disappointed, but I tried to encourage him. It wasn't like he'd ever done a lot of paddling in his life. Even though Randy was a maniac, he was strong, and he had canoed several times before.

As they prepared the sailboats for the final contest, the girls' cabins began arriving early for the free swim. It was bad enough that all the guys would watch me sail. Now the audience had just doubled.

I stared out across the lake. Mr. G had told us it was nearly six miles long. Did Jeremiah Potterfield really still live on the other side after all these years? How deep would it be out in the middle where we'd be sailing?

"Harry!"

"Huh?" I said, snapping out of my daydream. Leo was already in the sailboat.

"Are you ready? It's time to begin the race."

I nodded, zipping my life jacket. "Where do I sit?" The boat was flat with only a small, carved out part in the middle where Leo rested his feet.

"Right here," Leo said, patting the place next to him.

"Okay…" I slid onto the boat, grabbing the mast to keep my balance. The whole boat rocked unsteadily. I looked over at Leo. "Are you sure this thing can hold both of us?"

"Relax, it's fine."

He gave the thumbs up to the counselor on the dock, who shoved us off. Leo held a wooden tiller in his left hand. The stick was connected out the back to the rudder in the water. It seemed to work like a steering wheel. His other hand held a rope that was connected to the sail. As we turned toward the center of the lake, he pulled in the rope, and then secured it with a clamp.

"See? Piece of cake." Leo grinned as the wind blew through our hair. We skimmed along the surface of the water like a flat stone.

"How do you know all this?" I asked, watching the dock grow smaller behind us.

"My dad taught me. We vacation on a lake a lot like

this one. We spend a lot of time out on the water." He looked over at me and smiled. "Do you like it?"

"So far so good," I said, trying relax. It really was fun, especially since Leo knew what he was doing. I saw the other two sailboats further across the lake. "Not much of a race, though."

Leo laughed. "This is just the warm up. We have ten minutes to get the feel of things." He pointed to a series of orange buoys positioned around the lake in a wide square. "The race starts by the buoy nearest the docks. We do four laps around the square. First one finished wins."

I tried to imagine how we were going to navigate around the square with just the rudder and the sail. "So how does it work?"

Leo grinned. "Just do what I do okay? And watch your head." He unclamped the rope, and then pushed the rudder far to the side. The boat began to turn in the opposite direction. He slid across the foothold to the other side, and the sail started to swing across in the wind. "Careful," he said again.

I ducked before the metal frame holding the sail clocked me in the head.

"That's called 'coming about,'" Leo said, as he tightened the rope for the sail and clamped it back down. He pointed to a wind indicator at the top of the mast. "The direction of the wind determines how we position the sail.

"That's complicated," I said, trying to pay attention.

"Not really. You've just got to get the hang of it."

An air horn sounded from the dock and Leo repeated the whole turning process to bring us back to the starting line. At the first buoy, he turned the boat directly into the wind, taking us quickly to a near stop. When the boats were all close to the starting line, the air horn sounded once more. Harry adjusted the sails to catch the wind, and we shot off toward the second buoy.

CHAPTER SEVENTEEN

"Hang on!" Leo shouted, working the controls like a pro. I tried to move and duck whenever Leo told me to. The second person on a boat like that didn't seem to have much to do. That was fine with me.

At the end of the second loop, we were in the lead. All the campers were lined up on the swim dock and the shore, cheering us on when we passed the first buoy. While Leo navigated a straight line from buoy to buoy, the other boats were losing time zigzagging all over the lake. Leo waved confidently to the crowd as we finished the third lap. The rest of Cabin Eleven jumped up and down, waving their arms.

"You wanna try it?" Leo asked, sliding to the other side of the boat and handing me the line.

"What?" I cried. "No way! I don't know what to do."

Leo smiled wide. "Well, somebody better steer this thing, because I'm not."

I slid over and grabbed the wooden tiller tight in my hand. "Like this?" I asked. We seemed to be staying on course, but my heart was beating fast. It seemed like the temperature had suddenly increased by twenty degrees.

"Perfect!" said Leo, leaning back with the sun on his face. He closed his eyes. "Just head for the buoy."

"What are you doing?"

"I could use a nap."

"What? No!" I screamed, kicking him with my foot as we approached the third buoy. "Knock it off, will you? We have to turn. What do I do?"

Leo grinned and sat back up. "Okay, on the count of three, let the rope line out, slide the rudder all the way to the left, and move over to this side with me. And watch your head."

I tried to remember all the steps. What would happen if I hit the buoy? Would our boat splinter to pieces?

"Ready?" said Leo. "One, two, three! Hard a lee!"

I didn't know what the heck Leo was saying, but when he said three, I pushed the rudder as far as I could to the left. The boat spun to the right, the wind shifting to the other side of the sail.

The boat suddenly leaned far to the right. It was like Mr. Early's bus, careening across the highway on two wheels. Something was wrong. What had I forgotten?

"Let out the line!" Leo yelled as he clamored to hold on.

That's what I'd forgotten. I was supposed to loosen the sail rope before I turned. I reached up to unclamp the rope, but as I did, a gust of wind hit the sail. It pushed the boat even farther to its side. I was sure we were going to flip.

"Harry! Let out the line!" screamed Leo. His leg slipped over the edge, spraying me with water.

I yanked the rope loose. The sail released. The boat righted, flopping back into the water. Leo let go of the mast as the wind changed. The sail swung across the deck. Leo screamed as the boom knocked him over.

Before I even knew what had happened, he was gone. I spun around in horror to see Leo in the lake behind me.

He waved, floating securely in his lifejacket. "I'm okay! Keep going! You're going to win!"

Win? I didn't care about winning. I just cared about living. How could I sail without Leo in the boat?

I tried not to panic. Although I'd slowed down, somehow I was still headed straight for the final buoy. The screaming campers on the docks were growing closer and closer. I saw Nixon and Kareem waving me on.

That's when I realized I could actually do it. The next boat was gaining on me, but I tried to remember Leo's instructions. I looked up at the wind indicator, then tightened the sail. My speed immediately increased. The wind whipped through my hair. Sweat and water dripped down my face. I powered straight for the buoy.

The wooden tiller was gripped so tight in my hand I thought I might have blisters. Out of the corner of my eye I could see the next boat was only a few feet behind.

It was going to be close.

I gave the sail one final tug and gritted my teeth. I felt like a jockey in a horse race. The bow of the other boat drew even with my rudder.

Then I was at the buoy and the air horn blasted. The crowd on the dock cheered.

I'd done it. I'd won!

"Yeah!" I yelled at the top of my lungs, banging my palm down on the top of the boat. I was master of the ocean, sailor of the high seas, conqueror of the—

"Harry, watch out!" Nixon's voice screamed.

I looked ahead. I hadn't been holding my course. I was headed straight for the swim dock!

I panicked, swinging the rudder in the other direction. Once again, I forgot to let the sail out. The wind whipped the sail in one great burst. The boat toppled far to the side, plunging the mast into the lake.

I was catapulted. Flying through the air, I splashed into the water just ten feet from the swim dock.

Two lifeguards leaped from the docks. They grabbed my life jacked as I bobbed to the surface and pulled me onto the dock. I collapsed onto my back.

Kareem and Nixon ran over. They stared down at me, eyes wide with wonder, like I was a sea creature pulled from the deep.

"Are you all right, Harry?" Nixon asked.

I sat up slowly. "I think so."

"You won, Harry!" Kareem exclaimed, when he saw I wasn't dead.

"Harry!" another voice called from the water.

I stood and saw Leo coming toward the dock in a canoe with a counselor.

"Dude! That was awesome!" Leo screamed, scrambling onto the dock. He ran over and hugged me. "That was the most incredible thing I've ever seen, Harry."

I started laughing hard. "Pretty graceful, huh?" I exchanged high fives with him and the rest of the guys.

"That was the craziest sailing I've ever seen," said Anthony, shaking his head.

"You mean they don't do it like that at the 'Y' in Brooklyn?" I answered.

Anthony laughed. "They don't do it like that anywhere, man."

We walked off the dock as the counselors righted the sailboat and towed it back to shore. I passed Randy on the beach. He just shook his head.

"Nice work, Frog Legs."

"Hey, I won, didn't I?" I fired back.

He waved me off with his hand and we all joined the

crowd now gathered around the pavilion. Mr. G was adjusting the standings on the hanging board.

"Still in first place with nineteen points, is Cabin Six," Mr. G shouted, as he wrote the new numbers with chalk. Randy and his buddies all congratulated each other obnoxiously.

"But moving into second place, with sixteen points, after some fine swimming and a wild and daring sailing adventure on the high seas is…Cabin Eleven!"

"Woohoo!" we screamed at the top of our lungs as we high fived each other.

"Cabin Eleven rules!" shouted Kareem.

CHAPTER EIGHTEEN

Our whole cabin was psyched after moving into second place. I felt proud to have contributed, even if it was mostly by accident and had ended up as a near catastrophe. Mom says sometimes we just get lucky. After everything that had happened so far, I was happy to find a little luck for a change.

After dinner, the whole camp assembled to watch an outdoor movie. Mr. G projected the film on the side of the main building, and everyone gathered around with chairs or sleeping bags. He said that back when our parents and grandparents were kids, people went to drive-in movies all the time. They pulled their cars into rows in big fields in front of a giant outdoor screen.

That sounded weird. I told Mr. G that I'd rather just stream a movie on my tablet than go to that much effort. He just laughed.

The movie we were watching was *E.T.* James said he'd never seen it, which was hard to believe. I'd seen it at least ten times. It's one of Mom's favorites. She says it's a classic and makes us watch it whenever there's nothing else on.

The other guys in the cabin were excited too, so I tried to seem enthusiastic. I set up my sleeping bag next to theirs and we snacked on a box of Cheese-Its that Kareem had brought from home.

I think Randy must have been sick of watching *E.T.* as well, because about fifteen minutes in, I noticed him stand and tiptoe away from the group. I might not have thought much about it, except for the fact that I saw Marcy do the same thing. They both seemed to be heading toward the trail to the lake. I nudged Nixon, motioning toward his sister slinking away, but he was too into the movie to care.

I thought about how Randy had humiliated us on the docks during the swim test. How he'd scared us at the campfire. How he'd trashed our cabin and put a frog in my sleeping bag.

"I'll be right back," I whispered to Leo next to me, just as the kid in the movie was starting to feed E.T. some Reese's Pieces. Leo nodded, but he seemed to be caught up in the movie too.

I snuck off to the side, trying to look inconspicuous. As usual, Ryan wasn't paying attention, so no one noticed me leave. I saw two shadows fade into the trees on the trail so I followed them. I didn't have a flashlight, but after constantly running along the path for the last few days, I could almost find the way with my eyes closed.

I suspected Randy and Marcy were headed for some kind of romantic moment under the stars by the lake. It was disgusting. I didn't have a plan. I only knew that I wanted to get even. Randy always got distracted when he was with Marcy. Once I'd gotten back at him by using Marcy to lure him into our pitch-black dark basement. Maybe I could do something similar now.

I paused where the lake trail crossed with the cabins and shooting range trails. I listened, staring into the darkness. I tried to make out Randy and Marcy's forms through the moonlight. A girl's laugh broke the silence in the distance, and I turned toward the noise.

But then a branch snapped. It was much closer than the laugh. I froze. Had Randy seen me coming?

A low growl came from the bushes next to the trail. It started quietly, but then grew louder. What could be out there in the woods at night? It didn't sound like a bear. It was more like a cat. Did they have mountain lions in the Adirondacks? Nixon hadn't mentioned them on the bus, but who knew what wild beasts roamed these woods.

My heart beat faster. This was a really bad idea. I'd been so caught up in thinking about revenge that I hadn't considered what else I might run into. Maybe I should sprint back to the movie. Would Randy and Marcy hear me scream?

"Who's there?" I called, one foot already moving up the trail.

"Meow," came a sound. This time it sounded more like a house cat than a mountain lion. A shadow stepped from behind a tree and giggled. "I didn't scare you now, did I?"

"Ivy?" I said, trying not to sound scared. "What are you doing out here?"

She chuckled and patted my shoulder. "I saw you sneak off from the movie. I wondered what you were up to and took the short cut through the girls' cabins. I thought I might surprise you."

"You did," I muttered.

"Sorry. I thought it would be funny. Did you think I was a wild animal?"

"A mountain lion."

Ivy chuckled. "More likely it would have been a bobcat. So, what *are* you doing out here?"

I'd nearly forgotten about following Randy. I peered down the trail toward where I'd last heard them. "I was trying to play a trick on my brother. He snuck down there with Nixon's sister, Marcy."

"Is she his girlfriend?"

"Sometimes," I said. "They can't seem to decide."

"Well, I'm pretty good at sneaking up on people."

"I noticed."

"Can I help?"

"Well…" I wasn't sure I wanted Ivy to get in the middle of things with Randy, if only for her own protection.

"Which way did they go?"

"That way." I pointed down the left trail.

"They're probably on the swinging bridge. Ivy turned toward me. "Do you have a plan?"

"Well," I began. Truth was, I didn't have a plan. I'd been waiting to get there and see what happened. "Not yet."

"Sounds like you need my help," said Ivy, stepping up the trail. "Come on, let's go."

CHAPTER NINETEEN

Ivy headed off before I could object any further. If Randy saw me hanging out with her, it might make things even worse. Then again, maybe she could help me come up with an even better revenge plan. She'd certainly surprised me.

I jogged after her, watching for rocks and tree branches that might trip me up. Falling flat on my face would be the final insult. The trail turned and descended a small slope. The air was thick and filled with the sound of crickets and tree frogs.

"Is that a swamp?" I asked, smelling an odd odor.

"Yeah," chuckled Ivy. "It's so romantic."

As the trail flattened, the trees opened up into a clearing, revealing a dark sky full of stars. A small stream flowed beside us, leading to the edge of Lake Humphrey. Ivy was right. A small rope bridge spanned the gap where the trail crossed the stream, and that was exactly where Randy and Marcy had gone.

We crouched behind a tall evergreen, spying on Randy and Marcy in the center of the bridge.

"What are they doing?" I whispered.

"I think they're going to kiss." Ivy turned and made a funny gross face.

We were too far from the bridge to hear what they were saying, but the murmur of their voices rose and fell, mixing with an occasional laugh. I put my hand on the ground for balance. My finger touched a prickly pinecone, its edges rough on my hand.

I had an idea. I held the pinecone up to Ivy. She nodded and smiled. We gathered more from around our feet until we were fully stocked.

"We need to get closer," said Ivy. "Follow me and stay down." She snuck toward the edge of the marsh, the sounds of the night and Marcy and Randy's talking providing cover. Ivy paused twenty feet from the bridge behind a clump of Rhododendron bushes that hid us from view.

"Did you see me winning that canoe race?" Randy was boasting. I rolled my eyes and tossed a pinecone, purposely hitting the bridge a few feet from where they stood.

"What was that?" said Marcy as the pinecone bounced off the wood and rolled into the swamp.

"Huh?" said Randy, glancing at the bridge. "I didn't hear anything. Probably just a frog."

I nearly burst out laughing. A frog was closer than he thought.

Ivy fired a second pinecone, this time landing only a few feet from their legs. Marcy pushed Randy back and stood up straight against the rope railing. "That was not a frog."

Randy looked around cautiously. He must have heard it that time as well. I wondered if it was against camp rules to be down there without permission. I supposed we would all be in trouble if that were the case. Then Ivy let out one of her bobcat growls. It was so convincing that I nearly jumped, even though I knew it was her.

"Oh my gosh," whispered Marcy. "What was that?"

I held in a laugh and we tossed two more pinecones at the bridge. Ivy growled again, louder this time.

Marcy stepped toward the start of the bridge. "I'm going back to camp. I told you we shouldn't have come down here."

"It's okay," said Randy, grabbing her hand. I could tell he was nervous too, but he was trying to hide it. "It's probably just a raccoon or something." He wrapped his arms around her. "I'll protect you."

I nodded at Ivy and we fired all our remaining pinecones directly at the lovebirds on the bridge. It was hard to tell for sure, but I think one of mine hit Randy in the ear.

"Ow!" he screamed. "What the—"

Ivy let out another loud growl, which was enough to send Marcy scrambling to the start of the bridge near the trail. We couldn't hold it in any longer. Ivy and I burst out laughing.

"Hey!" Randy bellowed, staring down into the marsh. "Who is that?"

"Ribbit! Ribbit!" I yelled.

"Is that you, Harry?" He moved to the bridge railing closest to us, an evil scowl on his face. "Oh, I'm going to kill you!"

We stepped back from our hiding spot. It was fun scaring him, but I wasn't stupid. Randy was tough, and I didn't want him catching us.

"Let's get out of here!" I yelled.

As we turned to run, I looked over my shoulder. Marcy had walked off the bridge, but Randy wasn't taking the path. He had climbed right over the rope railing.

"Randy, leave them alone," called Marcy. "They're just being funny. Nixon, are you out there too?"

But Randy wasn't listening. He aimed to cut off our escape route. He leaped off the bridge, landing on a solid patch of ground in the marsh just five feet from where we stood.

"Run!" Ivy yelled, rushing forward onto the trail.

I tried to follow, but I tripped on a rock. I tumbled, my knee landing in the muddy ground. Randy's hand grabbed my foot. He pulled me back.

"Got you, Harry!" he cackled. "You're going to pay for this one."

CHAPTER TWENTY

"**H**arry, come on!" Ivy called from the trees.

This wasn't going at all like I'd planned. I tried not to panic.

"Let go of me!" I cried, trying to wriggle my foot from his grasp.

Randy grinned, turning his attention to the trail behind him. "Look what I caught, Marce. A real frog!"

"Randy, stop it!" Marcy called back from the edge of the bridge. "Just let him go."

In that split second, I saw my opening. Randy had humiliated me enough for one week. I pulled my leg toward my body, gritted my teeth, and then kicked back at him with as much force as I could muster. My kick must have caught him off balance, because when it hit him, he lost his grip on my foot. He flew backward, landing in the deeper part of the swamp, smacking into the mud with a splash.

"Ugh!" he moaned from the muck.

"Harry, come on!" Ivy called again from the woods. I jumped up and ran to the trail.

"Randy?" said Marcy, walking around the edge of the swamp. "Are you all right?"

In the moonlight, I watched Randy rise up out of the muddy swamp, dripping with grime; weeds stuck to his hair.

"Ahh!" he bellowed, sounding and looking like a Frankenstein monster.

Ivy and I burst out laughing from the tree line. I didn't know what was going to happen to us after all this, but in that moment, I didn't care. It was great to see Randy get what was coming to him.

"What's that on your neck?" Marcy said, standing on a rock to help him up. In the shadows it looked like splotches of mud were caked on his skin like polka dots.

Randy reached to his neck. He jerked his hand away. "Ahh, what is that?" he screamed.

Marcy leaned in closer. "Oh, my gosh, Randy. Take off your shirt!"

She helped him peel his shirt off over his head, and even from where we stood, we could see black splotches all over his torso.

"Leeches!" gasped Ivy.

"Ahh!" screamed Randy. "Get them off! Get them off!"

"Oh my gosh." I didn't know whether to laugh or not. I knew leeches were blood-suckers, but I wasn't sure how dangerous they were.

"Stand still!" screamed Marcy, reaching out tentatively to scrape the leeches off Randy's back. She turned toward us in the woods. "Help me you guys!"

Helping Randy had not been part of the plan. Of course, leeches hadn't been part of the plan either, but I didn't want to get too close even if Marcy was there.

Ivy didn't hesitate. "Come on," she said, pushing past me.

I cautiously followed, staring into the dark swamp water. How had all the leeches gotten on him so fast? When I touched one it felt slimy on my finger like a giant worm.

"Hold still, Randy," ordered Marcy. "We can't help you if you're squirming."

I don't think Randy was actually crying, but he was close to it. The time I had trapped him in our pitch-black dark basement he'd admitted he was scared and had cried then, but Marcy hadn't been standing there to see him.

We pulled as many leeches off Randy's chest and back as we could find. Thankfully he didn't try to attack us. Marcy reminded him that we were helping him whenever it looked like he might. I wasn't about to check him anywhere else, but they soon ran off to the cabins so Randy could shower. He shoved me out of the way, but I was pretty sure we were safe. At least for the moment.

"Well that was unexpected," Ivy said, after they'd left.

"Did you see the look on his face when he stood up out of the mud?" I started laughing again at the memory.

"It was perfect," said Ivy, laughing along with me.

"Thanks for your help."

"Don't mention it. It was fun."

"I'll have to start calling you Bobcat from now on," I said.

"That's better than Poison Ivy, I guess."

"Um…" I stumbled for words, somehow embarrassed that she knew people called her that.

"It's okay," she said, noticing my awkward expression. "I don't care."

I wanted to say that I knew all about getting called a mean nickname, but all that actually came out of my mouth was, "People are stupid."

"Yeah," Ivy said.

"Have people always called you that?"

"No, it started here last year when I had this argument with another girl in my cabin. She thought I'd purposefully caused our team to lose in the competition. She started telling everyone I was a traitor. Of course, I hadn't, but by then the nickname had stuck." She sighed. "It is kind of catchy, I suppose."

Once we were sure Randy was gone, we started walking back toward camp.

"Are you having a fun time here?" I asked.

"For the most part. I've been here twice before, but this year feels a little different."

"Different?" I asked. "How come?"

"It feels like after this everything is going to change. I'm probably going to be moving."

"Far away?"

"Kind of. A few towns over in Connecticut." She hesitated, then brushed her hair back and looked at me. "My parents are getting divorced."

"Oh," I said, not knowing exactly what more to say. I felt bad about asking in the first place. "Sorry."

"Yeah," she said as we reached the trail intersection and turned toward the dining hall. "I can't decide if I'm homesick or never want camp to end."

I nodded. "My dad goes away a lot for work. Sometimes it almost feels like my folks are divorced." I suddenly felt my cheeks burn hot in the darkness. I'd never said that to anyone before. I barely knew her, but somehow Ivy was easy to talk to.

"That sounds hard," Ivy replied. "Especially considering..."

"Considering what?"

"Considering that you have to live with Randy!" She giggled and patted me on the shoulder.

I laughed as we reached the clearing by the dining hall, which was shining bright with the projector's light. The movie was on the scene where the kids ride their bikes at night with E.T. sitting in the basket.

"Oh, I love this part!" Ivy squealed, sitting on an empty picnic table in the back.

I didn't know if she expected me to sit down with her or if I should go back to sit with my cabin, but I sat next to her anyway. I didn't have a lot of experience talking with girls, unless you counted talking to Marcy when I was over at Nixon's house, or my mom, or my teachers. Ivy leaned over and rested her head on my shoulder. I felt my heart beating fast, but it didn't seem too bad.

Like I said, I'd seen that movie maybe a dozen times, but somehow this time was different. Maybe it was watching it outside under the stars, or maybe it was sitting on the bench next to Ivy. But as we watched the final scenes, her head resting on my shoulder, it was like I was seeing it for the very first time.

CHAPTER TWENTY-ONE

T wenty-five pounds hadn't sounded like a whole lot. But as we marched across the courtyard, loaded down with our gear for the start of the hike, I started to wonder if Mr. G was right.

"This is kind of heavy," said Nixon, seeming to read my thoughts.

"Yeah," I answered.

"Man up, you guys," called Kareem, his canteen bouncing up and down from his pack in front of me. "Cabin Eleven has to be tough."

"Yeah, there's five competition points tied to the overnight," added Leo ahead of Kareem. "We can do this."

I wriggled my shoulders as something hard poked into my back. I tugged my pack straps tighter and tried to settle into the pace.

Ryan said we would hike as a large group for three miles up the side of Evergreen Mountain to the camp's usual site. We'd spend the night under the stars, and then hike back down in the morning. We took the trail behind the dining hall and crossed the leech-infested swamp on the swinging bridge. We hugged the west edge of the lake before veering to the left for the gradual climb up the mountain. We all trudged in a straight line, reminding me of the song the girls had been singing on the bus. We looked like an army of ants marching one by one, off into the woods.

The uphill path wasn't overly steep, but the weight on our backs made it harder. The ground was soft, padded with a thick layer of pine needles and moss. It reminded me of walking on a shaggy carpet or a playground with the cushy foam in case little kids fall off the monkey bars. As we walked deeper into the forest, it slowly morphed into a green, shadowy otherworld. Light streamed through the trees at odd angles where the leaves parted high above us.

After thirty minutes of hiking, it was mostly quiet among the boys as we settled in to a regular rhythm of walking on the soft ground. I wondered if it had been very different for the early explorers in America, wandering through the great forests and discovering new lands, uncertain what wild beast or native dweller might be lurking behind every tall tree.

I thought again of Nixon's talk of the snakes and bears that lived in the Adirondacks. Who knows what else he hadn't even mentioned? Surely a group of hikers this big would scare most things away. My eyes remained peeled just in case.

My attention was not just on wild beasts. Randy was up near the front of the march. After our prank at the swamp, it was probably only a matter of time until he mounted his own offensive. I knew he'd been embarrassed, particularly because it had happened in front of Marcy. I tried to decide which would be worse to deal with out in the woods, Randy, or a bear.

Some of the groups ahead of us stopped for a break at a bend in the trail. We happily slid our packs onto the ground with a groan. I leaned up against a tree. Leo stretched his fingers toward his shoelaces.

"How far are we?" asked James.

"About a mile in, I think," said Kareem. "It takes longer than you'd think when going uphill. It's not the same as walking around a track on flat ground."

"Whoa, look at that view," exclaimed Nixon, facing back down the hill. We'd all been so focused on climbing, we'd neglected to look behind us. Through an open section of the tree line we stared clear down to Lake Humphrey.

"Look, there's the pavilion. And there's the swim dock," said Anthony.

"Where?" asked Kareem.

"Right there," said Anthony, pointing down. "See the orange buoy from the boat races? The dock is just to the right of it."

"Oh yeah," nodded Kareem. "The site of Harry's infamous crash and splash."

All the guys cracked up.

"You're just jealous that I crashed so gracefully," I said, smiling.

"If that was graceful, I don't want to see awkward," said Kareem. "And poor Leo had to walk the plank!"

"Harry did a great job crossing the finish line," said Leo, grinning at me. "I needed a swim anyway."

The cabin ahead of us started to move, so we all pulled our packs back on. Mine seemed even heavier than it had before I'd taken it off. Maybe we shouldn't have rested.

"I can still see the look on your face on that runaway sailboat," said Kareem as he slipped on his pack.

"You thought you were a goner," added Nixon.

"We'd have all been goners if he crashed into the dock," laughed Kareem. He waved his hands in pretend panic.

"I never claimed to know how to sail," I said, laughing. I was still just thankful that I hadn't been killed. Making it across the finish line first was a bonus.

"True," said Leo. "I did talk you into it."

Kareem turned up the trail. "Just remind me to never get into a boat with you, Harry."

"Yeah, me neither," called Anthony.

"Or me," said James.

I shook my head. "Okay, I get it, guys. No more boats."

"I'll still get in a boat with you, Harry," called Leo.

"Thanks, Leo."

"Just not while it's in the water!"

Everyone laughed as we resumed our trek. Part of a long line of campers slowly ascending Evergreen Mountain.

CHAPTER TWENTY-TWO

The terrain grew rockier the further up the mountain we went. The trees had changed from the towering evergreens to a scattering of leafy branches and smaller shrubs. We moved more slowly, taking our time to make sure we didn't trip on the stones.

Ryan had checked on us after the break, but he quickly resumed his place up near the front with the other counselors. I'd have expected him, or someone, to stay in the back to make sure no one got lost or hurt, but he'd already proven that he cared more about talking to his friends than spending time with us. I wondered if Mr. G would approve of the job Ryan was doing, but he was back at camp with the girls, who had hiked earlier in the week.

"Hang on a second, guys," said Anthony from the back of the line. The rest of us paused.

"What's up?" asked Leo.

"Something's in my shoe." Anthony pulled off his pack.

"It's your foot, stupid," said Kareem.

Anthony frowned, sitting on a log. "No, it's a sharp rock or something. I have to get it out."

I leaned against another tree, afraid that if I took off my pack, I might not get it back on again. It felt heavier than a sleeping bag, a frying pan and food should.

I looked back down the hill. "How far do you think we've gone now?"

Leo shrugged. "Two miles? It's hard to tell."

I frowned, wiping the sweat from my forehead. It felt more like ten. I wondered if the others were as tired as I was.

"Come on, we have to catch up," said Nixon, looking up the trail.

"Oh, man," moaned Anthony, pulling off his shoe. A bright red splotch covered the sock over his big toe.

"What the heck did you do?" asked Kareem.

"Is that blood?" asked James.

"No, it's ketchup," said Anthony. "Yes, it's blood." He pulled off his sock and grimaced. "I knew it. A thorn."

"Ouch," said Leo. "Can you get it out?"

"I think so," said Anthony, crossing his leg to see the bottom of his foot. "Did anyone pack tweezers?"

"Oh, sure," said Kareem. "I've got Mom's medicine cabinet right here, hang on a minute."

"Dude, be nice," said Leo.

This was the first time I'd heard Kareem and Anthony arguing. I often felt like I was the only one with brother problems, but I guess all siblings get on each other's nerves sometimes.

Anthony glared at Kareem, then turned back toward his foot. "I thought maybe there would be some in the first aid kit or something."

"I think Ryan has that," Nixon said.

"Perfect," said Leo. "And when was the last time Ryan was around when we needed him?"

"Never," said James.

"Do you want me to get a saw?" asked Kareem. "We could just cut your foot off and Harry could carry you."

"Why me?" I asked, innocently.

Kareem grinned. "You're the overnight captain. Plus, I don't want to get his blood on me, man."

"Just hang on a minute, will you?" Anthony said, impatiently. He gritted his teeth and maneuvered his fingers together over his toe. "I think I can get it out." We gawked at him like he was about to pull a two-by-four out of his foot right in front of us.

"Got it!" he proclaimed, finally. He let out a long breath. "Whew."

"That might get infected," said Nixon.

Anthony looked up at him with an annoyed face. "Well, what do you want me to do? You heard Leo. Ryan has the first aid kit."

"I think you need to pee on it," said James.

We all turned and stared at him in surprise.

"What did you say?" asked Anthony, pulling his sock back on.

"You should pee on it. To keep the wound sterile," James explained. "I read it on the Internet one time."

We all started laughing. "I think you've lost your mind, James," said Anthony. "Stay the heck away from me."

James frowned. "I'm just trying to help."

Anthony stepped into his shoe with a grimace. "You wanna pee on something, you go behind the bushes. Got it?"

"That's not true, anyway," said Nixon.

"No kidding," said Anthony, standing up.

Nixon nodded. "It's a myth that urine can sterilize a wound. There's bacteria in your pee as well."

Like I said before, Nixon is good to have around. He's always full of useful knowledge like that.

"Okay, well now that we've established that no one is going to be peeing on Anthony's foot, can we get going?" asked Leo, nodding up the trail. "We're way behind."

Kareem shook his head at Anthony. "Nice going."

"Just shut up and start walking," Anthony shot back, shoving his brother forward.

We doubled our time up the trail, but after a few minutes, we still saw no sign of the rest of the group. We stopped at a fork in the path. Clouds had replaced the sunshine up above the trees. The air was growing cooler.

"Which way?" asked Kareem.

Leo looked both ways like he was crossing the street. "I don't know, I think it's this way," he said, pointing to the left. "But I'm not positive. The last time I was here, I just followed the rest of the group."

"Which we were supposed to be doing," said Kareem, glaring back at Anthony. "Maybe if you hadn't stopped to tie your shoe we'd still be with the group."

"I didn't tie my shoe," said Anthony. "You saw the blood. I had to get that thorn out."

"Whatever," muttered Kareem. He looked back at the trail. "So what do we do now?"

"Who's got the compass?" asked Leo.

"Me," I answered, remembering that the compass was in the side pocket of my pack. I pulled it out and held it flat in front of me.

"Which way is East?" asked Leo.

I struggled to recall what we'd learned about compasses in science class last year. Was that the day I left class early for a dentist appointment? My mind suddenly went blank as I stared at the plastic device in my hands.

"Harry?" asked Leo again.

"Uh," I said, turning the compass in my hands until the red marker stood still. The "E" for East was to the left. Mom says that deciding something is often better than just doing nothing. That had to be the right way.

"That way," I answered, pointing down the left fork.

"Left it is, then," said Leo, yanking on his straps. "Let's go."

I gulped and hoped we were headed the right direction.

Nixon caught up and tapped me on the shoulder. "Are you sure this is the right way?"

I nodded, trying to look confident. "That's what the compass said."

"Was that a rain drop?" asked James after we'd been walking a while.

"No," barked Kareem. "Keep walking."

James piped up again a minute later. "It's definitely raining."

Kareem shook his head. "Congratulations, James. What are you, a weather man or something?"

"I just thought you'd want to know," said James. "Geez."

"We're all out here, James," said Anthony. "We can tell if it's raining or not."

"Well it is," James repeated.

Anthony stopped and turned around menacingly.

"Come here, I'm gonna—" He acted like he was going to take a swing, sending James stepping backward.

"Hey, quit it," said Leo, stopping. "Let's take a break."

"We just took a break," said Kareem.

"Why haven't we caught up with the group yet?" asked Nixon.

I stepped up on a fallen log to get a better view, praying that the rest of the group would come into sight, but saw nothing.

"Did we take the wrong trail?" sighed Anthony, staring at me.

Leo shrugged. "I don't know. Harry, get the compass out again."

I pulled it back out, holding it flat. I breathed easier, seeing the red indicator still pointing at the "E" to the left.

Nixon looked over my shoulder. "Harry, you've got it upside down," he said, quietly. He took it from me and held it flat. "The red line is for magnetic North." He turned the compass so that the indicator lined up with the N. In that angle, the E was now to the right, not the left.

I closed my eyes. I'd led us in the wrong direction.

Everybody groaned. "You've gotta be kidding me," said Kareem, shaking his head.

"You mean we've been going the wrong way this whole time?" asked James.

"Not the whole time," I answered, trying to be positive. "Just since we came to that crossroads." I flashed a hesitant smile.

"Which was like forty-five minutes ago," said Kareem. "We are so lost." He sat down on the ground and shook his head. "This is a disaster."

"I'll tell you what it is," said James, quietly.

"What?" I asked.

James nodded solemnly. "It's the Cabin Eleven curse."

CHAPTER TWENTY-THREE

"There's no such thing as the curse, James," said Leo. As he said the word, a low rumble echoed from far away through the trees. I looked at the darkening sky, the rain now falling steadily on our heads.

"Was that thunder?" asked Nixon.

"Oh, great," said Kareem.

"I told you, it's the curse," moaned James.

"Dude, just shut up, okay?" said Kareem.

"So, what now?" I asked.

"We need to get under cover," said Leo.

"Anyone have a signal flare?" asked Anthony.

"Yeah," answered Kareem. "It's right here in my pack next to the tweezers."

"I meant that if we did, we could signal the others and—"

"We get it," said Kareem. He held his hands up. "No flares, sorry."

"I think we should turn around," said Leo. "We don't know where this trail leads. Maybe we can find the rest of the group if we get back to the intersection. If not, we need to find somewhere to wait out the storm."

"At least we're not in the middle of the wilderness or anything," said Kareem, waving at the trees. "Oh wait, yeah we are."

"All in favor of turning back, raise your hand," said Leo. I reluctantly raised my hand, along with Leo, Anthony, and James. "All in favor of continuing down the path?"

Kareem grinned and raised a lone hand. "Hey, we've come this far, who knows."

"That's only five votes," said Leo, looking around. "Where's Nixon?"

We all turned and glanced at the trees but didn't see him. "He was just here a second ago," said Anthony.

"Nixon?" I called out. It wasn't like him to just wander off.

"And they slowly started disappearing," whispered Kareem in a spooky voice. "The killer bear picked them off one by one until no one was left alive…"

"Knock it off, Kareem," said Anthony.

"Nixon!" I called into the forest. How I would

explain it to Marcy and his parents if Nixon never came back from camp?

"Up here!" came a voice from off the side of the trail. We turned and saw Nixon waving from a wide boulder up the hill.

"What are you doing?" called Kareem.

"The lake!" Nixon shouted back.

"Did he say lake?" asked Anthony.

"I think so," I answered, looking in the direction that Nixon was pointing. I climbed onto another log. On my tiptoes I saw a faint glimpse of water in the distance. How had we gotten back to the lake?

Nixon made his way back to us, his face in a wide smile. "The lake is in front of us. And I saw a building. It must be the camp."

"How could we be at the camp?" asked Anthony. "We've been hiking for miles away from the lake and the camp."

"Maybe we turned toward it when we took the wrong path," said Kareem. I thought he nodded at me, but maybe I was being paranoid.

"Should we go back?" asked James. "What about the overnight?"

"And the competition," moaned Kareem. "We're going to lose all those points if we don't show up."

Another crack of thunder boomed across the mountains, this time sounding closer.

"We can't stay out in this storm," said Leo, staring at the clouds. "I don't want to lose the points either, but we don't even know where the campsite is."

Everyone agreed with Leo, so we tightened our packs and cut through the woods toward the lake. It was harder walking without the path. The ground sloped downhill, so we turned our feet sideward and grabbed small saplings to avoid slipping in the wet leaves.

"This doesn't look like the woods around camp at all," said Anthony, glancing around the sloped terrain. "Do you think?"

Leo shook his head. "No, you're right. It doesn't."

"But there's Lake Humphrey," said Nixon, pointing to the water now in clear view ahead of us. "Is it a different lake?"

"Could be," said Leo. "Or just another part of ours."

"Look! Smoke!" said Nixon, pointing ahead at a small swirl drifting above the trees.

"Maybe it *is* the overnight campsite," I said, a glimmer of hope surging through my mind.

"Let's check it out," said Kareem.

We pushed forward through the woods with the lake on our left. The rain fell harder now. It occurred to me that it would be difficult for our group to be having a fire in the middle of the rainstorm, but I didn't say anything. Mom says maintaining a positive attitude is one of the most important parts of being successful, so I tried to stay optimistic.

Before long we saw that the smoke was coming from the chimney of a log cabin. It was nestled in a small, grass yard and faced the lake. I didn't recognize it as one of the camp buildings, but I hadn't been through every part of the camp yet. Maybe it was on the girls' side. I didn't see a car or a garage of any kind. Just a small metal boat tied to a ten-foot wooden dock at the edge of the grass. A motor was attached to the back of the boat, but it looked like a rowboat, only large enough to hold a person or two.

Kareem stopped behind a long woodpile.

"What's wrong?" asked James.

"Something's not right," Kareem answered.

"That's not the overnight site, and it's not the camp," said Leo.

"If it's not the camp, then what is it?" I asked, sinking into the leaves, my pack growing heavier and heavier.

"Maybe it's a ranger station," said Nixon. "I read that a state forest runs all around Camp Awonjahela."

"Look, there's a light on in the window," said Kareem.

"Well I'm getting soaked," said Anthony, wiping rain from his face. "You guys can stay out here, but I'm going inside." He took a step toward the cabin.

"Wait," hissed Leo, grabbing Anthony's arm.

"What?" said Anthony.

"I know whose house that is," Leo said slowly, peeking around the woodpile.

"Great," Anthony said, tugging at Leo's arm. "You can introduce us. Maybe they have a first aid kit for my foot."

"Whose house is it?" I asked.

"This is the other side of the lake. It has to be him," said Leo.

"Who?" asked Nixon.

"Jeremiah Potterfield."

CHAPTER TWENTY-FOUR

"Jeremiah Potterfield!" I exclaimed. "You mean he's real?"

"I thought that was just a legend," said Kareem, suddenly looking scared himself.

Leo nodded. "I told you, after the fire, he lived on the other side of the lake, and—"

"Shh!" hissed Anthony. "Get down. I see someone in the window."

We crouched lower behind the woodpile. I leaned around the side, squinting through the raindrops. I considered whether Leo's story could be true. Something had certainly happened to Cabin Seven, but I had no idea if there'd really been a fire, if a kid named Eddie Smith had really died, or if a camp director named Jeremiah Potterfield had been badly burned. He might not have even existed in the first place.

Could this really be his house? Would someone who was burned in a fire fifty years ago still seem hideous? I tried to imagine what old Jeremiah Potterfield might look like. Mom always says it isn't right to judge someone by the way they look on the outside. She says it's the inside that counts. I'm sure she's right, but that's not always easy to do. Some people are hideous on the inside and on the outside. Like Randy, for example.

Then the door opened and a huge German Shepherd walked into the yard. Kareem saw it at the same time I did.

"Oh, shoot," he muttered under his breath.

"Nobody move," I whispered, as the big dog froze in the center of the yard. Its nose lifted, smelling the air. He probably had sensed our presence and was plotting how to tear us to shreds, bit by bit.

"What is it?" asked Nixon, inching higher to see. His pack knocked the woodpile, sending several logs tumbling to the ground. The dog's head snapped toward us, ears alert, teeth bared.

A bolt of lightning flashed across the lake. Thunder shook the ground.

"We've gotta get out of here!" called Anthony.

"He's right," said Leo, standing up behind the woodpile. The dog burst into a series of fierce barks.

The door opened again. A figure in a long coat and

wide brimmed hat stepped out into the rain. He held something in his hand.

"He's got a gun!" whispered Nixon in my ear.

"Who's out there?" the man shouted, raising a shotgun toward the sky like he was about to fire. No one moved.

"Flush 'em out, Sampson," the man ordered, sending the dog on a beeline toward the woodpile.

"Run!" shouted Kareem, leaping from our hiding place. He only made it ten feet toward the lake before the dog cornered him against a tree, its teeth bared.

"Freeze right there!" the man yelled again, stepping into the yard.

We all moved next to Kareem, hands in the air like we were under arrest. I gulped, thinking about how wrong the week had suddenly gone. We were trapped in a deserted section of the forest between a killer attack dog and a grotesque loner.

"Sampson! Come!" the man ordered. He came toward us, a limp clear in his gait as he stepped across the yard. The dog gave a final growl, as if to say he'd been looking forward to ripping us to shreds.

We remained like statues, afraid to move. Another bolt of lightning pierced the sky as thunder simultaneously shook the ground.

"Well just don't stand there!" the man shouted over

the storm. "Get in the house before we all get fried." He turned on his heels toward the cabin, the dog at his side.

"What do we do?" said James, still standing with his hands up.

Leo took a tentative step toward the house. "I guess we follow him."

"In there?" asked Kareem. "Are you crazy?"

"What if he kills us?" said Nixon.

Leo shook his head as another crash of thunder boomed. "Would you rather stay out here?" He turned and ran toward the cabin. "Come on!"

CHAPTER TWENTY-FIVE

I t was dark inside the cabin. Several lamps were scattered across the open room, but they were turned off. A wood stove burned against the far wall with cast iron cooking pots on it. Flames were visible through the stove's small glass window. Shadows danced across the walls. The steady rain pounded on the roof over our heads. It was like we'd stepped back in time.

We happily shed our heavy packs, piling them inside the door. The man silently carried three wooden kitchen chairs into the main room, placing them in a row beside a worn-out-looking green couch. He handed out towels and motioned for us to sit down, even as we left puddles on the wooden floor. Sampson, the German Shepherd, lay in front of the stove, his head on the floor but eyes alert, watching these six intruders carefully.

"Storm knocked out the power," the man finally said.

He eased into the remaining open chair in the corner next to the stove. He removed his hat, but the shadows kept me from clearly seeing his face.

"Thanks for letting us in," said Leo.

The man grunted, glancing toward the window. "Nobody should be out in that kind of weather." His voice was crusty, but strong. "Especially a bunch of kids."

Lightning flashed. For an instant, I could see his face. The right side was a different color than the left, with scars stretching from his eye to the top of his shirt collar. I heard Nixon catch his breath on the couch next to me.

"You boys from the camp?" the man asked.

We nodded eagerly. Maybe if he knew we were from Camp Awonjahela, he wouldn't kill us. I looked for signs of a basement. Randy told me that in horror movies, the killer always has a basement. That's where they hide the bodies of victims, in the wall or under concrete.

"Is this still Lake Humphrey?" asked Leo. We all stretched our necks to catch a glance of the water out the window, as if the more things we could all agree upon, the more likely we'd be to stay alive.

"Uh, huh," the man answered. "You're a long way from camp, aren't ya?"

"We were hiking," said Kareem.

"For the overnight," added James, softly. "They'll be looking for us. Any minute now."

"Overnight, eh?" the man repeated, reaching down to

scratch Sampson's ear. The dog moaned softly, closing one eye, but the other watched us in case we decided to make a run for it.

"Don't remember them camping over on this side of the lake before," the man said. "You lost?"

We all nodded again quickly. "I had the compass upside down," I mumbled, feeling like I should say something.

"Humph," said the man. "What kind of camper doesn't know how to use a compass?"

"Yeah," I said, nodding. It sounded even stupider when I said it out loud. I wished I'd never gone to the dentist when Mrs. Jenkins was teaching about compasses. Maybe then we wouldn't be in this mess.

The next crash of thunder rattled the house so loudly we all nearly jumped out of our skins. Sampson let out a low whine. Apparently he didn't like the storm either.

"That was close!" cried Anthony.

"Keep your shorts on," said the man dryly. "It'll pass. Storms roll over these mountains with a fury this time of year, but they move quickly. Been that way for fifty years."

Leo cleared his throat. "Did you used to work at the camp, sir?" Everyone held their breath as he spoke the question that we'd all been too terrified to ask. "Are you Jeremiah Potterfield?"

The man was quiet for a moment. I started to wonder if he'd even heard Leo's question.

"Surprised anyone over there knows my name after all these years," he finally replied. He nodded gently. "That's me, son, but I haven't been to the camp in a very long time."

He leaned toward us, the faint light from the window revealing more of his face. My eyes bounced to the floor. I bet the others' did too. I was scared to stare at his scars. But I gradually raised my gaze. I tried to look in his eyes.

"Heard the stories, have you?" he said, seeming to read our minds.

We all nodded faintly.

"Yes, sir," replied Anthony.

Leo looked up bravely. "Is it true? What they say happened to Cabin Seven? Did a boy die in the fire?"

"Eddie Smith," said James.

Jeremiah Potterfield took a long deep breath, then settled back against the cushion of his chair. "It was a terrible thing, boys, that fire. A devastating loss for the whole camp and for that poor boy's family..." His voice trailed off. He touched his cheek with his index finger. "For me."

He looked back at us. "Camp is supposed to be filled with joy and laughter. I came up here to improve the lives of those young kids, to make a difference in the world. I wanted to promote character and goodness. I saw far too much evil in the war...all that killing. I wanted to do something good."

He stopped talking and stared out the window across the lake, as if he was reliving the tragedy of the fire all over again. I felt even worse for leading us in the wrong direction. If I hadn't, we wouldn't have barged into his house and brought back all those terrible memories.

"I almost died in that fire," he began again, slowly. "Was in the hospital for close to a year recovering. Burns over thirty percent of my body. Terrible skin grafts. Nothing you'd ever want to experience, fellas, let me tell you.

"When they released me, I tried to come back to the camp and work with the kids. But the way they looked at me, at my scars, like I was some kind of monster, I just couldn't take it. So, I moved back over here where I wouldn't bother anybody."

All at once I felt ashamed for looking away, for being part of another group of kids that told scary stories about him.

"But you saved the other kid, didn't you?" asked Kareem. "You were a hero."

Potterfield waved his arm. "Aren't any heroes in that story, boys. Only tragedy. If I'd gone to the left side of the cabin first, I would have found the other boy. No one would have died. It's something I've had to live with all my life."

No one spoke for a time after that. The rain fell in a rhythm on the rooftop. The storm gradually faded, moving across the lake to the other side of the mountain.

CHAPTER TWENTY-SIX

The lights suddenly flickered, then lit up the room. We all blinked our eyes at the brightness, stirring restlessly in our seats like we'd come out of a trance.

"Power's back," Potterfield announced, rising from his chair. Sampson stood and trailed him across the room. He punched at a telephone hanging on the wall, then held the receiver to his ear.

"Yeah, give me Mike Greenfield."

I was surprised to hear that the old man knew Mr. G's name. Surely Mr. G wasn't old enough to have worked at the camp when Potterfield was there. Maybe they stayed in touch somehow. Perhaps the rumor that Potterfield wandered over to the camp sometimes was true. It was a long way around the lake, though. The old man didn't seem like he was about to venture out on any long hikes, especially with his limp.

"Mike, it's Jeremiah…. Yeah, some storm…. No, I'm okay, thanks for asking. Listen, I have six of your campers." He paused. "What do you mean where? Right here in my house, that's where. They wandered in from the rain like a half dozen drowned rats. Sampson nearly tore 'em up." He glanced at us with a faint smile.

He paused again. "As far as I can tell." He turned his head toward us. "You're all fine, aren't ya, boys?"

We nodded quickly.

"Yeah," Potterfield said. "They're fine. A little water-logged, but I dried 'em off some." He paused. "Yeah, that would be great. Thanks, Mike…. No problem. We'll be here."

He hung up the phone. "Camp director's gonna drive over and pick you up in the van."

We nodded. I was happy to hear there was a plan for leaving. I wondered how long it would take Mr. G to drive around the lake.

"What about the overnight?" asked Anthony.

Kareem shook his head. "I think we can kiss our points goodbye."

Twenty minutes later, Sampson startled us with loud bark. An engine sounded from outside. A door shut and footsteps splashed up to the stoop.

"Mr. G!" Kareem exclaimed as Potterfield opened the door.

"Boys!" said Mr. G, shaking Potterfield's hand and

walking in. "I'm so glad you're okay. Ryan had radioed that you were missing, but everyone had to huddle at the shelter up on the mountain until the storm was over." He looked at Potterfield. "I see you've met my good friend Jeremiah."

"Yeah, he let us in from the storm," said James.

"You know each other?" I asked.

Mr. G chuckled. "Jeremiah has been a neighbor to Camp Awonjahela for many years." He looked down at us gently. "I suspect you may have heard a few stories."

"We had a good chat," said Potterfield.

"Well I'm glad," said Mr. G. "Sometimes the truth can seem a little more real after you see it in person. Right boys?"

We all nodded.

"Thanks a lot, Mr. Potterfield," said Leo, stepping forward and shaking the old man's hand.

We all echoed his thank you. I followed the others and shook his hand tentatively. It was rough and scarred from the burns. It was the closest I'd been to him since we'd entered the cabin. Though he had seemed scary, I could see that his eyes were friendly and kind.

"Happy to help, boys," Potterfield answered. "It's been a long time since any campers have been inside this house. It did me good, I think." He chuckled, then pointed to our packs piled in the corner. "But enough with all the mushy stuff. Get on back to the camp now where you belong."

"Sounds good to me," said Kareem, grabbing his pack.

We followed Kareem out into the yard with our packs. The rain had stopped, and the sunset was lighting up the sky over the lake.

"Hook any walleye lately, Jeremiah?" Mr. G pointed to the boat.

Potterfield grunted. "Nah, not much. Mostly bass. I keep trying, though. Mostly night fishin'. Can't seem to sleep much anymore. These boys are the biggest things I've caught lately." He cackled, a sly smile on his lips.

Mr. G laughed. "Well take care of yourself. Call me if you need anything, but I'll see you in a couple weeks." He reached down and pet the dog. "Good boy, Sampson."

"Thanks, Mike." Potterfield waved and closed the door behind us.

"Sounds like you boys had quite an adventure," said Mr. G, pulling the van slowly onto a narrow dirt trail.

"That's for sure," answered Leo.

I thought back to what Mr. G had said as we left. "Do you help take care of him?"

Mr. G smiled. "Oh, Jeremiah takes pretty good care of himself. And he's got Sampson there to help watch after him. But I've brought him groceries and supplies every couple of weeks for a few years now as he's gotten older."

"He seems nice," said Anthony.

Mr. G nodded. "He's a good man."

I sank into my seat by the window, watching the trees pass as the van circled back to the other side of the lake.

CHAPTER TWENTY-SEVEN

I t was nearly dark when we pulled into camp. It felt like we'd been gone for a month, rather than just several hours, after all we'd been through.

"Notice anything strange?" said Anthony, looking around as we pulled our packs from the back of the van.

"We're the only guys," said James.

"Is that good or bad?" asked Nixon awkwardly.

Mr. G laughed. "In a couple years you'll probably think that's a great thing, Nixon. But for tonight, why don't you all unpack and take some warm showers. I'll have food ready for you in the dining hall in about thirty minutes. Sound good?"

The mention of food made me realize I was starving. With all the excitement in the woods and at Jeremiah Potterfield's house, we'd forgotten all about dinner. We nodded and headed off toward our cabin.

A little later, it felt great to have showered and to not have to carry my backpack everywhere. I couldn't wait to eat and get to sleep.

"Hey stranger!" a familiar voice greeted me on the way back to the dining hall.

I turned to see Ivy smiling at me. "Oh, hi," I said. The movie had only been the night before, but so much had happened since then.

"What are you doing back? Did the overnight get canceled by the storm?"

I shook my head. "Nah, we kind of got off course and ended up on the other side of the mountain. Mr. G had to pick us up."

"Oh no!"

"Yeah, not ideal."

"Well," she said, smiling, "at least it's less time you have to spend with Randy. That's one positive."

I chuckled. "Good point."

"And now you're basically crashing a girls' camp," she added. "A lot of guys would kill for that."

"Yeah, that's what Mr. G said." My stomach growled and I nodded toward the dining hall. "I've gotta eat before he puts all the food away. I'll see you tomorrow?"

"Sounds good," said Ivy. "Maybe we'll be on the same team for Ultimate. They mix the boys and the girls, you know. Does your cabin still have a chance to win the competition?"

"I hope so," I said, remembering the big finale of the camp competition the next evening. "We were really close to first place before we got lost. I don't know what will happen now."

"I'm sure you'll do great," Ivy said, smiling. "Well, have a good night."

"Okay, see ya," I said, turning to the dining hall.

"Don't get lost!" she called.

* * *

IT WAS NICE HAVING THE BOYS' side of camp to ourselves. Without Ryan's snoring or a trumpet at dawn, I slept like a log. The overnighters wouldn't return until lunchtime, so we caught a late breakfast, then spent time down at the lake.

For a while, we had to share the water with several of the girls' cabins, but when they left for their next activity, the six of us from Cabin Eleven swam out to the diving platform. We laid flat on our backs on the wooden boards, soaking in the warm sunshine.

"This is better than hiking," said James.

"You can say that again," said Kareem.

"This is better than hiking," James repeated.

"Shut up." Kareem reached across and smacked James on the chest.

"Is it true they don't use tents on the overnight?" I asked.

"Did you notice any of us carrying tents?" replied Kareem.

"No, I guess not," I said.

"They were sleeping under the stars," said Anthony. "I kind of wish we could have done that. Like the old explorers, what were their names? Larry and Curley?"

We all cracked up. "I think those were part of the Three Stooges," said Leo.

"Lewis and Clark," said Nixon. "They mostly explored the western United States, though. Not New York."

"Whatever," said Anthony.

"It probably would have been muddy sleeping on the ground with all that rain though," said James.

"True," said Nixon.

"I'm happy not to be carrying that pack anymore," I said, rubbing my shoulders.

"Yeah," laughed Leo. "I think Mr. G needs a new scale. That was more than twenty-five pounds."

"Totally," agreed James.

We lay for a while in the sun, soaking in the rays and enjoying a chance to just relax. Despite some of the challenges this week had thrown at me, I was having a great time. I thought about how it was nice not worrying about Randy for a while. Ivy was right about that being a positive outcome of yesterday's drama.

When a cloud drifted in front of the sun, I sat up and looked back at the beach. It was empty except for a life-guard who was supposed to be keeping an eye on us, but didn't seem to be doing so.

"What are we going to do about the competition?" I asked.

Kareem sat up next to me and shook his head. "It's not good, man."

"But we were in second place," said Nixon. "Aren't we still close?"

"Not after yesterday," answered Kareem.

"The hike was worth five points," explained Leo grimly. "I don't know what Mr. G is going to do to our score, given what happened."

"We still hiked," James argued.

"Just not in the right direction," said Anthony.

"Sorry," I said again, still feeling bad for misreading the compass.

Leo patted me on the back. "Don't sweat it, Harry. It's not your fault."

"Yeah, if Anthony hadn't stopped to tie his shoe, we'd never have lost the group in the first place."

"Dude, it was a thorn," snapped Anthony. "I'd like to see you try to hike five hundred miles with a thorn the size of Texas in your shoe."

"Five hundred miles?" said Kareem.

"That's what it felt like," said Anthony.

"So, what's left in the competition?" asked Nixon.

"Just Capture the Flag," said James.

Leo turned and frowned. "Just Capture the Flag, James? That's kind of like saying it's just the Super Bowl or just the NBA Finals."

"It's huge, man," agreed Kareem. "The big conclusion to the entire competition."

"That's why it's called Ultimate," said Leo.

"How many points is it worth?" asked Nixon.

"Ten," Leo said.

"So how do we win?" I asked, thinking ahead. "It's the only way we can get back into the running, right?"

Leo nodded. "Assuming Mr. G gives us partial credit for the hike. If he doesn't, we'd be too far behind."

"I think he will," said Anthony. "He always seems fair."

We agreed that Mr. G would likely give us something, despite our finish. He was such a nice guy, perfectly suited to run a summer camp. I wondered if that was what Jeremiah Potterfield had been like before tragedy struck.

"We need a plan," said Kareem.

"I have some strategies from playing last year," said Leo. "But it all depends on who we're matched up with when they split the cabins."

I hoped we wouldn't be on the same team as Randy's cabin. We never worked well together, and we needed to get more points than his cabin if we were to move into first place.

We huddled on the floating swim dock, mapping out a strategy for victory.

CHAPTER TWENTY-EIGHT

M r. G stood on the picnic table outside the dining hall so everyone could see him. The entire camp was gathered around, buzzing with excitement.

"Ladies and gentlemen." Mr. G spoke through a megaphone. His voice was loud, but distorted. "Welcome to the final Camp Awonjahela competition event. Ultimate Capture the Flag!"

Everyone broke out in a loud cheer.

"Before we begin, I want to update everyone on the overall scores and go over the rules for the game. Listen carefully, as we'll be monitoring for any unsportsmanlike behavior or rule breaking."

I picked Randy out on the other side of the crowd. If anyone needed to be warned about unsportsmanlike behavior, it was him.

First, Mr. G walked through the scores for the girls' side of camp. Ivy's cabin was in third place and Marcy's was in second. Those were the only girls I knew, but it was good to see them doing well.

"On the boys' side," continued Mr. G, "currently in the lead, with twenty-seven points—Cabin Six."

Randy and his buddies raised their arms and shouted like a pack of gorillas.

"Boo!" I yelled, cupping my hands around my mouth. Mr. G looked my way and shook his head. I knew booing wasn't good sportsmanship, but I couldn't help it.

"In second place, with nineteen points, Cabin Eleven," Mr. G announced.

We dropped our heads. We'd dropped further back. Leo had convinced Mr. G to give us partial credit for the hike, and we'd been on time for meals, but apparently it hadn't been enough.

Kareem leaned over next to me. "We have to win this game."

Next, Mr. G reviewed the rules. The Red Team would be made up of boys' cabins Six, Nine, and Ten, plus girls' cabins One and Three. The Blue Team was cabins Eight and Eleven from the boys, plus girls' cabins Two, Four, and Five. Marcy was in Cabin Two and Ivy was in Cabin Five, so they were both on our Blue Team.

Even though Leo had summarized the rules on the

docks that morning, I listened carefully to Mr. G's explanation. I didn't want to mess anything else up that might cost us a win.

The basic rules went like this:

The camp property was split into two sections. The common area around the dining hall served as a dividing line and neutral zone. The Red Team's territory ran east of the dining hall from the boys' cabins to the edge of the beach, and to the far trail by the entrance road. The Blue Team had the other side of camp, west of the dining hall by the girls' cabins to the shooting range, and from the edge of the lake to the other side of the camp road entrance. It was a huge space, but there were more than thirty kids on each team, so we could spread out. Red and blue armbands identified the teams.

Each team had a flag, which Mr. G held up for us to see. They were thin, fabric beach towels, one red and one blue. Each team would place their flag somewhere in their territory, and it couldn't be moved during the game. It had to be within reach from the ground and be fully visible from at least one side. In other words, we couldn't stuff it in a rock crevice or hang it high in a treetop. The goal was to find the other team's flag, grab it, and then run back to your side without being tagged.

If you were tagged in enemy territory, you had to go to jail, a separate area within each team's side. You had to wait there until someone on your team ran in, tagged your hand, and set you free. Anyone freed from jail had a free pass back to the neutral zone. Guarding the jail or the flag was allowed, but no one could be closer than ten feet to their own flag or jail. If you were going to run, you had to turn on your flashlight to keep anyone from getting hurt.

Leo said the strategy was what made it the most fun. Some kids needed to be Guards on our side to tag players from the other team and prevent jailbreaks. Others needed to be Attackers and sneak into enemy territory to look for the flag. Scouts did a little bit of everything, like a midfielder in soccer. It sounded complicated, but Leo said it wasn't hard once things got started.

As we organized in the neutral area, I saw Randy and Cole strutting across the courtyard like their Red Team had already won. He caught my glance and flashed an evil grin, slowly running his index finger across his throat.

"He's so weird," said Ivy, standing next to me.

"Yeah," I said at the understatement of the year.

Everyone was split up into roles. From our cabin, Kareem and Anthony were Attackers, Leo and James were Guards, and Nixon and I were Scouts. I liked the fact that I could be flexible. The rest of the Blue cabins were divided up too, matching a balanced number of boys and girls and older and younger cabins across the roles.

Ivy was also a Scout. "Cool, we can help each other." She reached up and gave me a fist bump. "Good luck."

I smiled. "You too."

"Campers, you have five minutes to hide your flag."
Mr. G's voice boomed through the megaphone. "On the
second signal, you may begin crossing into each other's
territory."

He blasted an air horn, the sound echoing through
the woods. We all cheered, our adrenaline pumping.
Then we scattered through the woods; disappearing into
the night.

CHAPTER TWENTY-NINE

Most of the Blue Team ran together, moving deep into the heart of our territory. Leo knew a perfect spot to hide the flag near the entrance road. He convinced the older guys from Cabin Eight to hang it from a rock face that was only accessible from one side. It was legal, but Attackers would have to come at it from behind, making it easier to defend. While they hid the flag, James and three girls from Ivy's cabin set up the jail at the flagpole outside the girls' cabins.

When the second air horn blast sounded to start the game, Kareem, Anthony and our other Attackers raced off to find the Red Team flag. Their flashlight beams bounced through the trees as they ran on our side, but they switched them off before they crept stealthily into enemy territory.

Nixon, Ivy, and I walked with the other scouts toward

the neutral zone. We fanned out to cover more ground, working like a security force on high alert. I eyed the trees warily, knowing that each shadow or snapping twig might be a Red Attacker.

"It's kind of spooky out here," said Nixon as we crept along.

"It's the same woods as always," said Ivy.

A voice called out on our left. Two lights flashed on. One of our other scouts chased a Red invader.

"Got you!" the voice yelled.

Followed by a reluctant, "Aw, man," from the captured player.

"Haul him off to jail!" called Ivy.

"Where are we headed?" asked Nixon.

"Let's go down along the edge of the lake," I suggested. "I'll bet they hid their flag in the back just like we did."

At the edge of the neutral zone, Ivy crouched down. "Shh. We must be very quiet. We're hunting wabbits."

Nixon tried not to laugh and give away our position. We followed her lead, sinking down and listening for sounds before moving slowly through the trees. The night was eerily quiet, especially knowing that the woods were swarming with campers. I imagined being in a real army, in a real war; my face camouflaged black and green as I sneaked into enemy territory.

"Harry, you coming?" called Nixon, waving from up ahead.

I stood, but suddenly a voice cried out. "Get him!"

I looked up to see a girl on the Red Team running at me full speed. I spun, avoiding her tag. I ran toward Nixon and Ivy. We tore down the trail toward the lake.

"You have to turn your lights on when you're running!" our pursuer called, her own light bouncing as she chased us. We reluctantly flipped on our flashlights, knowing it would make us visible to any other Red Guards within range.

"We have to shake them," said Ivy. "Let's split up. Meet by your cabin, okay?"

I nodded as she veered left. I kept going straight, but the pursuing light followed Nixon to the right. I grimaced a few seconds later when a voice called out that Nixon had been tagged. I turned off my light and sank into the undergrowth. I watched from the shadows as Nixon was marched off to the Red Team's jail. I felt bad that Nixon had been captured, but there was nothing I could do.

I rose and slowly headed toward my cabin. The woods looked somehow different but yet the same as I moved along in the darkness. I heard voices approaching at the trail intersection. I hid in the shadows just as three Red players ran past. I heard Randy's voice barking out orders to another group coming up behind them. I tried to blend further into the bushes. If he found me, it would be worse than a regular capture.

Suddenly a hand covered my mouth.

"Shh," a voice whispered in my ear.

I turned to see Ivy crouched next to me.

"I didn't scare you again, did I?"

I shook my head even as my heart pounded. I wondered if she might really be part bobcat because of the way she could sneak through the woods. I pointed silently to the trail just as Randy and Cole paused in front of us.

"I'm sure they put their flag in the back by the cliff," said Cole. "That's what I'd do."

"I'm going to cut through the rifle range," said Randy. "I'll come in to the cliff from the other side of the access road."

"That's outside the boundaries," said Cole.

I could picture Randy's devilish grin through the darkness. "Exactly," he cackled. "It's the perfect way to get in, undetected. Why risk dodging all the Guards when I can go the easy way? No one will know."

"Nice," said Cole as they high fived each other.

"I'll grab the flag while you lead the others in a mad rush from the front," said Randy. "They'll never see it coming."

"And we're still celebrating later, right?" said Cole.

"Sure, you'll bring the rest of it down to the pavilion

on the beach?"

"Yup. It'll be smoking," said Cole. "Let's go!" He took off up the trail toward the neutral zone. Randy snuck toward the rifle range.

"How can he do that? It's cheating," said Ivy when they'd gone.

"It's Randy," I explained, matter-of-factly. I was used to his bad sportsmanship. Nothing he did surprised me anymore.

"What are they talking about, celebrating down on the beach?" Ivy asked. "Are they going for a late-night swim?"

"I don't know. But we have to warn Leo and protect the flag."

"Right," said Ivy, standing up. "Let's go."

We moved back up the trail toward the neutral zone, keeping watch for Cole and the other Red players.

At the trail intersection, we heard voices calling out. "Help, save us!"

Ivy stopped short and pointed toward the lake. "The jail! It must be on the beach. We have to free them."

I nodded. "Come on."

We snuck along the tree line until we saw a group of Blue players standing in the volleyball court. Two of them looked like Nixon and Anthony. Four Red Guards stood further out on the sand, scanning the trees for rescuers. I motioned for Ivy to go to the right while I went left. If we both ran from the trees at the same time, we just might reach the jail without being captured.

I moved into position on the other side of the beach. I counted to three and bolted across the sand, hoping Ivy was following my lead. Out of the corner of my eye I saw her running from the trees too. One of the defenders screamed a warning about Ivy. At the last second the guard saw me too, but she slipped in the sand as she tried to change directions.

Anthony saw me coming and reached out his hand.

"Got you!" I cried, tagging his hand.

"Freedom!" we all screamed, laughing and running. We flaunted our free passage at the Guards who began arguing with each other over whose fault it was that we had broken through.

"Nice job," said Anthony, slapping me on the back, "and good diversion, Ivy!"

We turned and ran back up the trail toward Blue territory. I told Anthony what we'd heard from Randy by the cabins, and we beelined it to Leo and our flag.

I hoped there was still time.

CHAPTER THIRTY

By the time we reached the neutral zone, things had turned crazy. Voices were screaming amidst a blur of tags and captures on both sides. In the shadows, I could barely tell team Red from Blue, or which was winning or losing.

"This is chaos!" cried Nixon as we jogged past the dining hall.

A wild yell rang out across the neutral zone. A dozen lights flicked on at once then stormed into Blue territory like a swarm of bees.

"They're starting the attack!" yelled Ivy.

We raced forward, trying to cut the fastest route to Leo and the flag. The woods were a blur of bouncing lights and screams as we flew through the trees. We reached the boulder and the Blue flag just before the attack.

"They're coming!" we yelled ahead.

Marcy was guarding the right side. She flashed her light in our eyes. "Who goes there?"

"It's us," Nixon called. "Cole's leading a full-on attack! There's tons of them."

"Where's Leo?" I asked.

Marcy pointed around the back of the rock face. I ran toward him as Nixon and Ivy helped Marcy line up the other Guards to face the attack.

"What is it?" asked Leo.

"Randy!" I called, out of breath.

"What? Where is he?"

I pointed into the dark trees behind the boulder. "He's coming up the back through the rifle range."

"That's out of bounds. He can't do that!" argued Leo.

I nodded but quickly explained what we'd heard. Just then, Cole's attack surged around the boulder. Ivy, Nixon, and our other Guards were in hot pursuit. I looked back for the flag.

It was gone.

Randy lunged away from the rock face, tucking the blue fabric under his arm.

"The flag!" I screamed.

"Get him!" yelled Leo, as Red Attackers swarmed all around.

Randy handed the flag off to Cole like a football.

Cole leaped over a log with the flag then sprinted through the trees toward the neutral zone.

"No!" Leo cried, chasing after him.

Randy raised his arms in victory. Then he turned to me, grinning. "And now, time for some unfinished business."

For a second, I was frozen. Technically, I could tag him, since he was in Blue territory, but I didn't think he cared anymore. I knew he was still mad about the swinging bridge and the leeches.

I spun on my heel and ran, pushing the branches and leaves from my face. I didn't care which direction I was headed. Only that I was moving away from Randy.

"I'm going to get you," he bellowed, crashing through the forest behind me.

I was out of bounds, but I didn't care. A blast of the air horn sounded through the woods from the dining hall. Cole must have made it across the neutral zone with the Blue flag without being tagged.

The game was over. We'd lost.

I stopped and turned around, shining my light in Randy's eyes. "The game's over, Randy. Leave me alone! You cheated, but you won, okay? Are you happy?"

"This is a new game, Frog Legs," he cackled. "Because you made me look like a fool in front of Marcy."

"You did that just fine all by yourself," I shouted back, trying to find my nerve.

But he kept coming. "Now you're going to pay."

I wondered how I got myself in such a mess. Why had I come to Camp Awonjahela? It was Nixon's fault. He'd invited me. I never should have said yes.

I reached the edge of the ravine that separated the rifle range and the lake. The ground was still wet from the storm. My foot hit a slick spot and my legs flew out from under me. I toppled down into the ravine, barely missing a dark tree with my head.

For a moment, I lay still in the leaves, catching my breath. I could hear Randy stepping down the hill.

"You can't run forever, Frog Legs!" Randy called.

I had no choice but to get up. I took off again through the woods toward the lake.

I ran until I reached the water, then I followed the shoreline toward the beach. Maybe someone would be there. They could help me, or at least keep Randy in check. Ultimate was over and everyone was supposed to go back to their cabins. Surely someone would notice I was missing.

My side ached from running. I couldn't hear Randy behind me any longer. The darkness had swallowed him. Maybe Randy had given up.

When I saw the shadow of the pavilion on the beach, I slowed to a walk. I knew where I was now. I could take the trail back to the cabins.

I was halfway across the beach when sparks suddenly shot out of the lifeguard's stand.

BANG! BANG! BANG!

Firecrackers popped loudly in the night. I crouched down, covering my ears. Where had they come from?

"Gotcha!" Randy cried, grabbing my shoulders. He shoved me down into the sand.

"You're late," came a voice from the pavilion.

"Sorry, I had to catch a frog along the way," Randy cackled, stepping on my back with his foot and pushing me harder into the sand. He shined his flashlight to reveal Cole walking toward us with a shiny red box under his arm.

Fireworks.

"Harry?" a voice called from the edge of the trail.

Randy took his foot off my back and shined his flashlight toward the trees.

It was Ivy.

"Oh, this is perfect. Your little girlfriend's come to save you." He shook his head in the glow of the flashlight. "Didn't Dad tell you to stay away from the Poison Ivy, Frog Legs?" He pointed his light back in Ivy's eyes. "This is family business. Take a hike."

"What are you going to do, Randy?" I scrambled away from him and stood, brushing the sand from my clothes. Ivy ran up next to me. I wished she hadn't gotten in the middle of things. "Mom's going to notice if I don't come back from camp you know."

"Oh, don't worry, you'll make it home," said Randy. "I'll take good care of you."

Cole lit another pack of firecrackers and threw them down at our feet. "Catch!" He and Randy laughed and ran toward the trees.

BANG! BANG! BANG! BANG!

Ivy screamed and we both jumped away from the firecrackers in the sand. Sparks flew against our legs, the air smelling pungent.

"That's really smart, guys!" Ivy yelled. "What's the matter with you?"

"What's the matter with you?" Cole repeated, mocking Ivy's voice.

"Are you okay?" I asked, rubbing my ankles which were stinging from the flying sand and sparks.

"Yeah."

I looked at her through the shadows. "What are you even doing down here?"

"When you didn't show up in the neutral zone at the end of the game, I thought maybe Randy had done something to you."

"How did you know we were on the beach?"

"I remembered Cole talking about celebrating on the beach after the game and thought maybe you would be here."

I'd forgotten all about that in the craziness of running from Randy. "You probably should have stayed away." I nodded toward the shadows. "They're out of control."

Ivy peered into the darkness. "What are they doing over there?"

I heard Randy and Cole laughing, but I couldn't see them. "I don't know, but it can't be good."

As I spoke, a loud "thwoop" sound came from the edge of the woods and a bright orange spark shot into the sky. A burst of light filled the beach as a firework exploded just overhead. Sparks rained down onto the sand.

"Yeah!" cried Cole from the edge of the woods.

"Nice one," said Randy.

"Are you crazy?" yelled Ivy. "You're going to kill somebody!"

"Knock it off, Randy," I said.

"Oh, that was nothing," Cole's voice answered back. I saw his shadow scurry along the tree line, then saw the glow of a flame.

I turned again to Ivy. "We have to get past them."

Suddenly, multiple streaks of light poured into the sky like rockets, one after another. Pops and bangs and whistles filled the air. Cole must have set the whole box on fire.

"Oh, jeez!" shouted Randy.

"Come on, let's get out of here!" yelled Cole.

Fireworks were flying in every direction. Some shot high into the sky, others were streaking across the beach.

"Watch out!" screamed Ivy as a rocket zoomed just above our heads.

There was a crash. I turned around to see the pavilion in flames. Fire was consuming the streamers and the welcome banner hanging from the ceiling. The wooden scoreboard that tracked the competition points was smoldering. Smoke was everywhere.

I looked back at the trees but Randy and Cole were gone. Ivy was running to the lake, a bucket in her hand.

"What are you doing?" I yelled to her.

"We have to put it out before it's too late," she screamed. "Help me!"

I helped her lug the water from the lake. We stood just inside the edge of the pavilion and dumped it into the fire, but it barely made a difference. The flames were spreading rapidly. The pavilion was old and the wood roof seemed to catch fire easily.

"It's too much!" I called, feeling the heat on my face. "We can't do it."

I turned to grab her arm, when a cracking sound came from above us. A burning rope landed by our feet. We dodged out of the way, but Ivy collided straight into a wooden beam, smacking her head. She staggered, then fell to the ground.

"Ivy!" I called, crouching over her.

Another crash sounded above me. I looked up just in time to see the heavy, wooden scoreboard falling. It cracked hard on my head.

Then everything went black.

CHAPTER THIRTY-ONE

Barking. That's the first thing I heard.

I coughed, then I opened my eyes. Fire and smoke was all around me. I was lying inside the pavilion. I heard more barking.

Then I saw Ivy lying next to me on the ground. A piece of wood was on top of her, the competition score-board. She wasn't moving. A dog was barking insistently just beyond the flames.

"Ivy!" I screamed, pulling myself up. The dog was racing back and forth on the sand. What was it doing there?

I crawled next to Ivy, staying low, the roof above us sizzling with flames. We had to get out. The board was hot, but I pushed it off her.

The dog jumped through the flames, bursting into the pavilion. It licked my face.

Sampson! But how?

"Ivy!" I yelled again, pulling her up.

She coughed and slowly opened her eyes. "Harry? What's happening?"

"We have to get out of here!" I screamed, coughing repeatedly from the smoke. One of the roof sections crashed to the ground across from us.

Sampson was barking and dancing on the edge of the pavilion, looking for a way out. I heard yelling now. Dark figures were running down the beach.

"Harry!" a voice called. It was Randy.

"In here!" I shouted, helping Ivy to her feet. I waved my hands and could see my brother's horrified face on the other side of the flames.

Another face appeared. An old man. Potterfield!

He threw a rope into the pavilion. "Follow the rope. You have to jump over the flames!" he called. "Come on, Sampson!"

The dog hesitated, but then leaped out to the sand. I picked up the rope, my other arm under Ivy's shoulder. "Come on, we have to go!" I yelled.

The smoke was thick and the flames were almost touching us, but I pulled the rope tight and we lunged past a burning picnic bench. We kept moving forward until we reached the sand.

"I got you, Harry!" Randy yelled, grabbing hold of

us. Potterfield pulled Ivy from my grasp and guided us further from the pavilion.

I looked back just in time to see the rest of the roof tumble to the ground. Flames engulfed the very spot where we'd been standing.

A crowd surged toward us from the trail. Mr. G raced over, his eyes wide. "Is everyone out? Is there anyone else in the pavilion?"

I shook my head. I tried to find my voice. "No!" I coughed. "It was just us."

Mr. G's face eased and he ran toward the fire. He barked out orders as a group of counselors cleared all the remaining objects from around the pavilion so nothing else would catch fire.

Ivy collapsed into the sand. I huddled next to her. "Are you okay?"

She nodded and tucked her knees under her chin. Her face was black from the smoke and charred wood.

Sampson sat next to us. His tongue licked my face. "Hey, boy," I said.

I looked up at Jeremiah Potterfield. His face reflected the glow of the fire, his eyes fixed on the flames. "What are you doing here?"

"Saw the fireworks from the water," he replied.

"All the way across the lake?"

"Nah, from the boat. We were fishing. Sampson started barking. He could tell something was wrong before I even saw the flames. He jumped off the boat as we motored close and ran to you."

Sampson whined at his name and nuzzled his nose against my face. I patted his head, trying to process everything. "I heard him barking. I think I was unconscious."

"My God," Potterfield muttered, still staring at the flames. "I can't believe I'm seeing this again."

"We're okay," I told him. "We all got out."

He nodded slowly. But I wondered if he really understood.

Ivy looked at Sampson and Mr. Potterfield, her eyes showing confusion. I realized she probably had no idea who they were.

"He saved us," she said slowly.

I nodded. "I think he did."

How had everything gone so wrong? Randy had chased me through the woods after Capture the Flag. He and Cole started shooting off fireworks. They hit the pavilion. They ran away. We had tried to help and ended up almost dead because of it.

Randy walked back to us with Mr. G. "Are you sure you're okay?" Randy asked, bending down next to Ivy and me.

"No thanks to you," I answered, my anger rising. "We could have been killed!" When he turned away, I jumped up. "What's the matter with you, anyway?" I screamed in his face. "Why do you have to be such an idiot?"

My blood was boiling now. It was one thing for him to pick on me, but this time he'd gone too far. We could have died.

"Nobody likes you," I screamed, tears suddenly pouring down my cheeks. "I wish you weren't even my brother!"

"It's okay, Harry," said Ivy, standing next to me. "We're all right."

"I'm sorry—" Randy muttered, shaking his head. "We were just messing around." He looked back at the smoldering remains of the pavilion. "I never meant for any of this to happen."

"Just get out of here, will you?" I said. "You've done more than enough."

I wanted to punch him in the face with all my strength, but Mr. G stepped between us. "Harry, Ivy, let's get you both up to the clinic."

"Harry, wait—" Randy put his hand softly on my shoulder.

"No!" I screamed, jerking away. "Don't touch me."

CHAPTER THIRTY-TWO

Nurse Trella examined us carefully up in the clinic. She said we'd be okay, but that we had inhaled a lot of smoke. She gave Ivy an ice pack for her head where she'd hit the beam, but she didn't think either of us had any concussion. She told us to take it easy, just in case.

"Capture the Flag is always my busiest night of the week," she said, "but this is taking things too far." She wrapped Ivy and me in hugs. "I'm just so thankful you're both okay."

"Us too," replied Ivy.

We passed Mr. G as he walked to the camp office. He told us that things had been stabilized down on the beach. The fire was out. He was calling a late-night gathering for all campers in the dining hall. But first he was going to speak with Randy and Cole in his office. From the look on his face, I could tell they were not going to like what he had to say.

A girl from Ivy's cabin was there to walk her back to clean up. Leo was waiting for me. I gave him a brief rundown of what had happened as we walked. He couldn't believe it.

While I washed up in the bathroom, Leo told the boys' cabins about the gathering, and then we all walked back up to the dining hall. I filled the rest of Cabin Eleven in on everything that had happened.

Most of the camp was already in the dining hall when we sat down. Wild rumors were flying about the events on the beach. Everyone was looking at me and whispering. I didn't know if they still thought I was cursed, or if they were just happy I'd survived. I picked Ivy out from the other side of the room and waved.

Mr. G wasn't there yet. I wondered if he was still speaking with Randy and Cole. I wished I could see Randy squirm under Mr. G's questions. I'd originally hoped that Mr. G would find out Randy had cheated in Ultimate, but things had turned so much worse.

With everything going on, I hadn't even thought about the competition, but that was what most of the campers were still talking about. Mr. G had declared the Red Team the winners, but only on a conditional basis. He'd wanted to speak to us first since Randy and I hadn't returned. Everyone on the

Blue Team was claiming that the Red Team had cheated.

"You'll have to talk to him," said Kareem. "It's not fair what Randy did."

"It's gone way beyond the normal competition," said Leo, leaning over.

The dining hall door finally opened. Mr. G walked in with Cole and Randy following behind. All the campers buzzed with whispers at the sight of them. All of a sudden, a wet tongue licked my ear. I spun around to see Sampson perched next to me on the bench.

"Whoa!" the guys all exclaimed next to me.

The volume in the room increased as the kids saw the dog. Then Sampson jumped down and walked over to where Jeremiah Potterfield was sitting on a chair next to Mr. G. A hush grew over the crowd. Everyone eyed the mysterious man and the dog on the platform.

You could hear a pin drop as Mr. G took the microphone. "Well that's what I call coming to attention. Thank you, campers.

"I know it's late, but I think it's important that we come together tonight and address what has happened. As many of you know, Camp Awonjahela has been here for fifty-seven years. Thousands of boys and girls, just like yourselves, have sat in this room for meals, swam in the lake, and slept in our cabins. I've been Camp Director here for just seven of those years, but the staff and I have always worked hard to promote our core values of fun, friendship, and adventure. You may have noticed that I left out the fourth of our core tenants just now. Safety. Most of the time, it's a value that goes unnoticed."

Mr. G paused. He stared out at the room. I think he looked at me, then at Ivy. I wondered if he was getting emotional. I realized there must be a lot of responsibility on his shoulders to take care of so many campers each summer.

"Fifty years ago, there was a terrible tragedy here at the camp. A fire was started in one of the cabins, Cabin Seven, which involved a young boy named Eddie Smith. Eddie was twelve years old. He loved to play football. He loved to go camping. But he and another camper were playing with a lighter and things got out of hand. Eddie died that night.

"A brave camp director was walking by and went in to help. He nearly lost his own life and was severely injured, but he rescued the second boy. I know many of you have heard stories about him over the years, and I realized recently that I should have done more to connect him with our camp community. That man is Mr. Jeremiah Potterfield, and he's here with us on the stage tonight."

Mr. G turned and shook Potterfield's hand. The room of campers buzzed with whispers and surprise. I looked over at Randy and Cole sitting alone at the counselors' corner table. They both looked down at the floor.

I didn't know what to think any more. I'm sure Randy was truthful on the beach, saying that he hadn't meant for anyone to get hurt. And I was pretty sure they had been Cole's fireworks. Mom and Dad would never have allowed Randy to bring something like that along. But he had let things get totally out of control.

"Tonight," continued Mr. G, "we nearly had another tragedy. Tonight, some of you ignored our safety tenant. There was a fire in the pavilion down on the beach, caused by the irresponsible use of fireworks. You all know that fireworks are not allowed here at camp, expressly for this reason. Too many things can go wrong. Thankfully, tonight we escaped with only minor injuries. There was no loss of life. But it reminded me about how dangerous things can quickly become when someone ignores the rules.

"In another miracle, Mr. Potterfield and his dog, Sampson, were fishing on the lake. They'd motored closer when the fireworks exploded. Then they saw the smoke and the flames. They rescued two of our campers who had innocently become trapped in the fire. Pavilions can be rebuilt. Lost lives cannot be.

"For your continued acts of bravery, I am again, Jeremiah, forever grateful. Thank you from all of Camp Awonjahela. We are truly in your debt."

Mr. G turned and began clapping his hands. He nodded to us, and before long everyone was standing, the room erupting in applause. I felt the tears flow down my face again, but even with the dozens of eyes staring at me, I didn't care.

CHAPTER THIRTY-THREE

I slept right through trumpet call. Nixon had to shake me before I'd open my eyes the next morning. I'd been running through the woods all night in my dreams, hunting for Red flags and dodging flames. It took me a minute to wake up enough to remember where I was. It was departure day, and I was suddenly very ready to go home.

At breakfast, it was my turn again to wait on our table. Leo tried to say he'd take over for me, but I didn't mind. This time I got the drinks first.

"Who wants bug juice?" I announced, placing the pitcher in the middle of the table.

"Bug juice!" they all cheered.

I smiled, thinking about how much I'd learned since the start of camp. It felt good to laugh about something silly like juice after everything that had happened.

I saw Ivy in the food line. She smiled and gestured for me to come in line next to her, giving me a quick hug as I did.

"How are you?" I asked.

"Starving," she said.

I grinned. "I don't know why. It's been so boring around here, don't you think?"

"I can't believe today's the last day." She sighed. "It's gone fast, don't you think?"

"Yeah," I replied. "In most ways." Camp had gone quickly, all things considered. Not only had all the drama occurred, but I felt like I'd gotten to know her and the guys pretty well in a short amount of time. I think everything happens faster when you spend the whole day with friends.

"Are you going to miss it?" I asked, then laughed. "I mean, besides the fire and almost dying, of course."

Ivy laughed too, then tilted her head. "Yeah. Especially with everything happening at home. I just wish things could stay the same, you know?"

"Yeah," I answered.

The truth was, I didn't really know. I didn't know how hard it would be for her to go home to a family that was splitting up and moving to a new town. Despite all the challenges at my house, I didn't envy her. I tried to think of something to make her feel better as we stepped into the kitchen.

"Are you online? We could stay in touch."

She looked back and me and smiled. "Absolutely, that would be great!" She picked up a pen from the bulletin board on the wall. "Here, hold out your arm."

"My arm? Why?"

She giggled. "Just do it."

I glanced around to make sure nobody was looking then held my arm out toward her. She started writing on it with the pen.

"What are you doing?"

"Just hold still." The pen tickled, but I tried not to move.

"There," she proclaimed. "All done."

I tried to read what she'd scribbled.

POISONIVY123

She grinned and grabbed a food tray. "That's my ID. It's through my mom's account, but look me up, okay?"

"Deal," I said, as we parted and headed back to our tables with our food.

As I passed out breakfast, Leo smirked like he'd seen me talking to Ivy and was going to say something about it. I started to protest, but he put his finger to his lips to indicate he would stay quiet about it. Maybe everyone had learned something this week about judging people based on rumors or appearances.

The microphone squawked through the PA system.

We looked up to see Mr. G standing at the front of the room, a paper in his hand.

He had checked with me before breakfast after everything that had happened at the pavilion. I'd told him what Randy had done at the end of Ultimate. I explained what Ivy and I had heard him say and then how we'd seen him come from outside the perimeter to take the flag and hand it to Cole.

All that seemed less important after the fire, but Mr. G wasn't surprised by it either. He said Randy had admitted to going out of bounds. He told me that Cole's parents had been called and were picking him up later that morning since he'd brought fireworks to the camp. Randy would go home on the bus as planned, but I suspected he might not be invited back next year.

"Good morning, campers," said Mr. G. "It's been quite a week, and I'm sure you're all anxious to get home. Before you do, there's one unfinished piece of business. With all the excitement last night, we didn't get to finalize the standings for the camp competition. And while everyone's safety is much more important than a game, I thought you'd like to know the final results."

All the cabins cheered loudly. The guys around the table sat poised with anticipation.

"Hopefully, he believed you," said Nixon.

"He has to," said Leo.

"Don't worry," I said. "Even Mr. G could see Randy's a cheat."

"After speaking to players from both teams, I've decided that the Red Team intentionally went outside the boundaries during Ultimate Capture the Flag. As a result, those Red Team players have been disqualified. Since those players were directly connected to the taking of the Blue flag, I'm declaring the Blue Team the winners."

"Yes!" cried Kareem. Half the room cheered and the other half moaned at the decision.

"Wait," said Leo, quieting our cabin. "We have to see about the competition points."

"And now for the final standings of the camp competition," Mr. G said, holding up the sheet of paper. The crowd hushed once more, eager for the news.

"First the girls' cabins. In third place, with twenty-three points, Cabin One." He paused for a smattering of applause. "In second place, with twenty-five points, Cabin Four." A cheer went up as the girls figured out who had won their side of the competition. "Which means that first place, with twenty-eight points, goes to Cabin Two! Congratulations, ladies."

I looked behind us and saw a group of middle school girls from Marcy's cabin stand up and hug each other.

"And now for the boys' competition," said Mr. G.

"Woo, woo, woo," all the boys chanted around the room.

I suddenly had butterflies in my stomach. Until the fire, the competition had been all we were thinking about. I felt the competitive fire resurface in my mind.

"In third place, with twenty-seven points, Cabin Eight," said Mr. G. We all froze, knowing that we must be in the final two places. I looked across the room, but I couldn't find Randy's face. Had he been late for any meals? I wondered if we'd done enough to pass his cabin.

"In second place, with twenty-eight points…Cabin Six."

A cry erupted around our table as we stared at each other in surprise. My mouth dropped open.

"Which means that first place, with twenty-nine points, is Cabin Eleven! Congratulations, boys!"

"Woohoo!" screamed Kareem.

We all leaped from our seats and hugged each other, jumping up and down. We'd won!

"As a special treat, our two winning cabins may now head into the kitchen for ice cream sundaes."

"Wow!" said James, stepping toward the kitchen

"Hang on, James," said Leo.

James turned back and frowned. "But it's ice cream for breakfast, Leo."

"I know, but we have to do something first." He reached out and poured bug juice into six cups.

"What's going on?" I asked.

Kareem handed me a cup.

"It's a toast," said Leo. "To our victory!"

"Oh, right," said James. "To breaking the curse!"

"Dude, what have we said about that!" said Kareem.

"No, for once, James is right," said Leo, raising his cup. "We broke the curse by winning the competition and finding out the truth about Jeremiah Potterfield."

"Maybe you're right," Kareem shrugged. We all raised our cups high into the air.

"To Cabin Eleven!" shouted Leo.

"Cabin Eleven!" we all cheered, tapping our cups together joyfully.

"Now where's the ice cream?" yelled James. We all laughed and ran to the kitchen.

"So, what do you think, Harry?" asked Leo as we waited for ice cream. "Same time next year?"

I grinned, thinking about the fun adventures we'd had. I never truly thought we had a chance to really win. It just goes to show that trying hard can pay off sometimes. Having a cheating brother who disqualifies himself doesn't hurt either, but that's beside the point. I saw Randy walking out of the dining hall. A year was a long time to live with a brother like him, but maybe I could make it if I knew I was coming back.

I smiled at Leo. "Absolutely!"

CHAPTER THIRTY-FOUR

R yan made us pack up and clean the cabin from top to bottom after we returned from breakfast. He said he was a counselor for the next week too and didn't want to live in our filth. We all felt sorry for the new batch of Cabin Eleven kids who would be stuck with his bad attitude.

At least they wouldn't have to deal with Randy. Then again, maybe there were other kids like me with older brothers who loved to make their lives miserable. I don't think anyone could be quite as bad as Randy, but who knows, the world's a crazy place.

Afterward, we carried our bags up to the dining hall courtyard. Luggage was lined up in rows and grouped by bus.

"Look, there's Mr. Early!" Nixon said, pointing to the parking lot.

"He's on time?" I said, laughing.

"Is that a new bus?"

"Looks like it. Thank goodness."

"Ready to go home?" Marcy asked Nixon as she set her bag next to his. Randy was with her and he set his bags next to mine. I tensed, half-expecting him to reach over and dump my bag on the ground.

"Yes," replied Nixon. "Hopefully the ride back is a little less eventful."

"Congratulations on the winning the competition, guys," Marcy added, smiling.

"Thanks," Nixon answered.

"You too," I said, remembering that Marcy's cabin had come in first for the girls.

Marcy nudged Randy with her elbow and nodded toward me.

"Uh, Frog—" he started. She poked him harder in the ribs. "I mean, Harry."

"Yeah?"

He looked again at Marcy, but then continued. "I'm really sorry about the beach. We should never have been shooting off those fireworks. And I shouldn't have chased you. I never meant for you or Ivy to get hurt. It was stupid." He stuck his hand out like he wanted me to shake it.

I eyed him warily, waiting for the punch line, or more

likely just the punch, but he seemed serious. I cautiously raised my hand. We shook awkwardly.

I knew he probably meant it. That's the thing about most of his tormenting. He never actually thinks about hurting anyone. He just thinks it's entertaining for him.

I suppose my throwing pinecones at him wasn't very nice either, but it wasn't like I set the bridge on fire. How was I to know he'd fall in the swamp and get covered with nasty leeches? Mom says two wrongs don't make a right and all that, but living with a brother like Randy can do a lot to mix things up in a kid's head. I wonder what she'll say when she hears he nearly killed me in a fire.

"Truce?" Randy said, smiling.

I took a deep breath. We'd had these kinds of truces before. They worked for a while, but before long we would be back to our normal ways. It was kind of pointless, but I supposed something was better than nothing. Maybe the seriousness of the fire would make him more careful.

"Truce," I repeated, wondering if it would even last through the bus ride home.

Maybe, if I was lucky, it could go on for a few days. Mom and Dad would be around, and they would have just found out about everything that had happened at camp. Who knows, maybe it could last through the rest of the summer.

That was probably asking too much, but I tried to

stay positive. Peace treaties only work when both sides follow the rules, and with Randy around, nothing was truly safe.

But when you're in a brother war, like me, you take any moment of peace you can get.

ACKNOWLEDGMENTS

I have vivid childhood memories of going off to a week of summer camp deep in the Adirondack mountains. Later, in college, I spent a summer as a counselor at another camp in the mountains of Massachusetts. There's a little bit of magic in being away from home and school, living in the woods, and experiencing life with other kids your age.

This is my second *Brother Wars* book, and it's been fun to write more about the misadventures of Harry and Randy. There is something universal about the love/hate relationship between brothers. It tends to be a recurring theme in my books since I have three active sons. Thankfully their battles haven't (yet) escalated to the point of Harry and Randy's, but they have their moments.

As always, I have many people to thank as I put this new story into the world. First and foremost my family—

Mary, Matthew, Josh, and Aaron for believing in me and being patient with my writing. Thanks to my parents for always being supportive even when I announce I'm changing careers.

Special thanks for my camp memories and experiences from Word of Life, Northern Frontier, and Grotonwood. Thanks to my friends at Richmond Children's Writers, James River Writers, The Smarter Artist Summit, Ryan and Alicia for their guidance, Mary at The Little Bookshop, Sue, Jenny, and Lacy at B&N, and Jill, Melanie, and Juliana at bbgb.

Thanks to my colleagues at Medscape, particularly Rej, Jeff, and my team for twenty years of challenges, friendship, and experience that I use in my writing life every day.

Thanks to Kim for her edits, Dane for his artwork, and the many educators I've met along the way at local schools, especially Kyle King, Kristen Cross, Shannon Hyman, Mary Jo Krufka, Audrey Surma, and Tara Hannon.

Last but not least, thank you to the many young readers whose wonder, smiles, and enthusiasm have made this whole endeavor worthwhile.

ABOUT THE AUTHOR

Steven K. Smith is the author of *The Virginia Mysteries* and *Brother Wars* series for middle grade readers. He lives with his wife, three sons, and a golden retriever named Charlie, in Richmond, Virginia.

For more information:

www.stevenksmith.net

steve@myboys3.com

ALSO BY STEVEN K. SMITH

The Virginia Mysteries:

Summer of the Woods

Mystery on Church Hill

Ghosts of Belle Isle

Secret of the Staircase

Midnight at the Mansion

Shadows at Jamestown

Spies at Mount Vernon

Brother Wars:

Brother Wars

Cabin Eleven

The Big Apple

DID YOU ENJOY CABIN ELEVEN?

Would You ... Review?

Online reviews are crucial for indie authors like me. They help bring credibility and make books more discoverable by new readers. No matter where you purchased your book, if you could take a few moments and give an honest review at one of the following websites, I'd be so grateful.

Amazon.com
BarnesandNoble.com
Goodreads.com

Thank you and thanks for reading!

Steve